Family
Feeling

Patsy Collins

The author can be found at
www.patsycollins.uk

ISBN: 978-1-914339-37-0

Contents

1. Crazy Cat Lady

"O. M. G.! Have you gone completely mad?" Tara asked, the moment she stepped into Caitlin's bedsit.

Caitlin didn't answer; she doubted she'd manage plausible deniability when surrounded by cat-shaped cushions, especially not these particular cat shaped cushions. "When did you start speaking in acronyms?" she asked instead.

"F. Y. I. I'm using abbreviations, not acronyms."

"Whatever. How long have you been doing it?"

"Since you turned into the crazy cat lady."

"I haven't. You know I'm not keeping them and they're all on eBay."

"So you said – and that you've got a buyer for one!" Clearly Tara wasn't convinced.

"Actually they're buying them all." Which had sounded odd even to Caitlin, especially when she'd received a message which didn't even provide a real name, just their online username. They'd offered to pay in cash and collect in person. Whoever it was had a good buyer rating, so was probably genuine, but Caitlin had asked her much braver sister to be there when they arrived.

"T. B. H. they sounds as barking mad as you." Tara sank onto the sofa, only to leap up again as the cushions erupted into furious yapping.

"L. O. L.," Caitlin said.

"It's not funny."

"Yes it is! Well, this one was the first time." Caitlin threw an extremely fluffy Persian towards her sister.

As Tara caught it, the sound device inside was activated and it gave a deep 'woof'.

Caitlin smiled as she recalled the first time she'd heard it, in a local gift shop. Although amused, she hadn't actually considered buying the cat and was looking round for something more sensible when she'd noticed what was going on at the till.

An angry customer had brandished a ginger tabby, which emitted a distinctly canine sound with every sudden movement.

Damian, the reason Caitlin was in the shop at all, was trying to placate the customer. Even, "That's why they're just a pound each and described as seconds, sir," sounded sexy in his voice.

Caitlin could hardly wait for Damian to ask if there was anything he could do for her. She wouldn't answer of course, she'd be far too shy for that and would just put her purchase on the counter and offer a twenty pound note. She'd made a point of getting one, so she could be close to him for a moment longer as he sorted out her change.

"What will you be trying to sell me next?" the customer had snapped. "Sausage dogs miaowing, goldfish singing like canaries?"

Damian assured the man he wouldn't, although he did seem to be struggling not to laugh.

Finally the customer had accepted his refund and stomped out. He tried slamming the door, but the closure device wouldn't let him.

Damian had given Caitlin such a lovely smile. "What can

I do for you?"

As he'd uttered the longed for phrase, Caitlin's nerves kicked in. She put the cushion on the counter and fumbled in her purse for the note.

"Are you sure you want this?" Damian had asked. He'd put his hand on the Persian, releasing another woof. "Apparently they were made by mistake and the company who produced them also have a batch of Dobermans who purr."

Caitlin had giggled. "It's probably a good thing you didn't tell Mr Angry that."

Damian's hand brushed hers as he gave her the change and receipt, but thankfully she managed not to jump, or drop anything.

"Is it for a gift?" he asked.

"Ummm ..."

"If they don't like it, just bring it back. I'll be very happy to see you again... er... and give you a full refund."

Caitlin wasn't absolutely sure if she was just hearing what she wanted to, but it had seemed as though he meant the bit about being happy to see her again. So she'd gone back... and bought a growling Siamese. And then a tortoiseshell, followed by a black one with white feet and tail tip, both of which yapped.

Each time she'd returned to the shop, she and Damian had said a little more to each other. Each time she fell a little further in love with him and each time she dared to hope he was beginning to feel something for her.

Caitlin told Tara the whole story, ending with, "I'm almost sure that if I could let him know I'm not just going in to buy cat cushions then he'd ask me out."

"Hmmm and in the meantime you'll buy a dozen more and be smothered to death by them all!"

"No, honestly I won't. For one thing there's only one left in the shop and for another someone will be here in a minute to buy all these."

"Why would anyone want them?"

"I. D. K." Caitlin said. "Want a coffee while we wait?"

"Yeah, thanks."

As Caitlin was busy with the kettle when a young man rang the doorbell just a few minutes later, Tara answered it.

"Hi. I'm Shopboy98... here about the cushions."

As Caitlin had said she didn't know why anyone would want them, Tara asked him.

"Because there's this lovely girl who keeps coming into the shop to buy them. I've nearly got up the courage to ask her out, but I'm worried we'll sell out first," Damian said.

"Then you'd better come in and speak to my sister A.S.A.P.," Tara said.

2. Bank Holiday Monday

When her elderly relative's letter arrived Alison squealed, "Aunt Cecilia's coming over for the wedding!"

It would be like stepping back into her childhood. The cousin getting married lived in the same Cornish village as Alison's grandparents had. School holidays were spent there, all the cousins together. They'd had so much fun. Aunt Cecilia visited from her home in South Africa most years and spoilt the children even more than Grandma and Granddad had.

Paul said, "Are you going to invite her here? She was good to us when we went there, besides I rather like the old girl."

"I'll ask. I hope she agrees but I expect she'll be in demand."

The popular lady wrote back to say she was staying part of the time with other relations. 'If it isn't too much trouble, could I travel back from the wedding with you and stay a day or two before flying home?'

Alison agreed and asked Aunt Cecilia if there was anywhere she'd especially like to visit, or anything she'd like to do. She'd listed attractions near Portsmouth, suggested getting a Hovercraft to the Isle of Wight, train to London, even a ferry to France. Aunt Cecilia replied that she'd discovered there'd be a Bank Holiday during her stay. 'I'd love a picnic at Lee-on-the-Solent just like when I was a child'.

"A picnic?" Alison exclaimed when she read the letter. "I was hoping to do something really special for her."

"You asked what she wanted," Paul pointed out.

"But why Lee-on-the-Solent? There's nothing there, not even sand!"

"I don't suppose there was much more when she was a girl."

A search on Google revealed there used to be a pier, tower and Art Deco cinema complex, none of which remained.

Paul didn't see the problem. "She just said she'd like a picnic, nothing about piers."

"I know, but she wanted it to be like her childhood."

"You can't turn back time, love. Just do the best you can."

"I suppose so… I'll just have to make it a really special picnic."

There wouldn't be much chance after the wedding, so Alison organised everything she could in advance. She arranged with a neighbour to borrow their gazebo and deckchairs so Aunt Cecilia could sit comfortably whatever the weather. She ordered a marvellous picnic including fresh strawberries, luxury ice cream, chocolate eclairs, smoked salmon and wine from a very up-market delicatessen. She even hired a Punch and Judy man.

"No brass band and Red Arrows fly past?" Paul joked when she told him.

Alison ignored that and packed ready for the wedding.

The Devon village had changed a lot since Alison was there as a child.

Aunt Cecilia gave one tiny sigh. "Nothing is ever quite as you remembered when you go back." Her usual sunny smile quickly returned. "Still, we needn't let that stop us enjoying ourselves!"

The wedding was wonderful. Great company, food, drink, location. Great everything. Alison's picnic would seem pathetic after that.

Before they left she called the delicatessen. "Is it too late to change my order?"

"No, that's OK."

"I'd like king prawns, please. The very biggest you can get and a bottle of champagne."

It wasn't much of an improvement, so throughout the four hour drive home, Alison wracked her brain for further ideas.

"I think we're going to have to pull over for a while," Paul said. "The car's coughing and spluttering worse than a donkey with a sore throat."

Donkeys! There were probably donkey rides on the beach when Aunt Cecilia was a girl.

"No, don't stop," Alison pleaded. There was a riding stables not far from where they lived, maybe they'd have a donkey she could borrow?

"It's overheating, love. If we don't let it cool down it might stop altogether."

"I could do with a cup of tea," Aunt Cecilia said. "Let's take the opportunity to visit somewhere we'd otherwise have driven straight past."

Oh dear! Alison had been so preoccupied with making the picnic perfect she'd totally disregarded Cecilia's current comfort. She felt even worse when her relative insisted on paying for their refreshments.

The lack of donkeys didn't seem important the following

day while dashing through the rain to load the deckchairs into the car. They didn't get off the driveway before it made a horrible noise and stopped.

"I'm so sorry, Aunt Cecilia I think we're going to have to get the bus."

"I hope it's a double decker. You get such a good view of everything."

Before Alison could reply her phone rang. It was the lady from the delicatessen.

"Sorry we've been held up," Alison explained.

"Shall we leave your order with the Punch and Judy man?"

"Please. Is there a cool box so the ice cream doesn't melt?"

"There isn't any ice cream. That was on the order you cancelled."

"I didn't! The prawns and champagne were supposed to be as well as the rest not instead!"

Alison cut off the woman's apologies and pulled open the kitchen cupboards. She flung together jam sandwiches, apples, packets of crisps, and a bottle of orange squash then caught up with Paul and Aunt Cecilia at the bus stop.

Paul gave a running commentary during the journey, as though conducting a guided tour, which Aunt Cecilia seemed to enjoy.

When they arrived at Lee-on-the-Solent the rain had almost been blown away by an icy wind. The Punch and Judy man was being cautioned for causing a disturbance. Apparently after drinking the champagne, which he insisted he'd been given not stolen, he'd put on a decidedly adult version of his show.

They declined his offer of a repeat performance and huddled together in the bus shelter eating slightly crumpled sandwiches and taking turns to drink squash from the bottle.

"Alison my dear, I really can't believe this," Aunt Cecilia said.

"Neither can I, I'm so ..."

"After I asked you to organise a picnic for me, I almost immediately regretted it. I was sure you could never recreate the Bank Holiday Monday picnics I remembered as a child, but you've captured the experience perfectly! Now pass those crisps will you, dear. They go so well with the prawns."

3. Sun, Sea, Sand

They woke quite late on the first day of the holiday to sun streaming through their windows and excited children wanting to know when they could go to the beach.

"Right after breakfast!" Natalie said.

The kids opted for their usual brand of cornflakes and she and Stuart had bacon sandwiches with Heinz ketchup. The glass of orange juice they washed it down with was Spanish though. They'd had to make it something quick as they'd been warned the kitchen would be out of action from 9.30 and the builders would start their noisy work soon after.

They'd hardly started gathering together sunscreen and swimwear and trying to decipher the local bus timetable when the sound of building work started. Natalie couldn't help wincing.

"We did know it would be like this," Stuart pointed out.

Natalie shrugged. "Yes and it's cheap." She saw Stuart's expression. "Ah well, we're stuck with it for the next couple of weeks. Might as well make the most of it. Come on kids, let's go."

The children's enthusiasm was a good distraction to the chaos behind them and luckily the bus not only arrived within minutes but had a driver who cheerily responded to their greetings and issued tickets without requiring any more instructions than, 'the beach please'.

The journey was quite interesting, taking them through the

town and allowing them a brief glimpse into the lives of the local people. On the way, Natalie reflected on the conversation which had led them to take this particular holiday.

Natalie's brother had just returned after a cheap package deal to Spain.

"Everyone spoke English, Premiership football matches were on in all the pubs which sold all the familiar brands of beer alongside the local cerveza and vino. Full English breakfast was available in every hotel and copies of British papers to read with it."

"Told you you'd hate it," Natalie said.

"Actually no. It was rather fun. Maybe because we didn't get our hopes up too much. Relaxing, good weather, no stress and we didn't have to have fish and chips every night. It was just as easy to get paella and frittata."

"And by doing that instead of the kind of thing we usually do, we saved enough to get a new suite and decorate the lounge," his wife added.

"We could do something like that," Stuart suggested after they'd gone.

"Maybe." The trip quite appealed and she and Stuart could do with a holiday; they'd not had one in the six years since their eldest was born. "But we can't do that and have work done on the house and that's more important."

Unlike her childless brother, taking even the cheapest of package holidays with their kids would use up most of their savings. Natalie and Stuart's home needed updating and not just because the furnishings weren't the latest fashion.

"Spending quality time with the kids is just as important. Giving them happy memories and letting them experience something new."

"I suppose."

"And we both work hard. A couple of weeks of fresh air and exercise instead of the office and the daily commute, relaxing evenings drinking wine and talking instead of housework and slumping in front of the TV would do us good."

"OK, you've convinced me."

They'd spent quite some time looking round for the very best deal and picking a fortnight in the school holidays which they could both take off work, but eventually everything was sorted out.

"Have fun and don't forget to send us a postcard!" her brother said as he handed her a few folded notes. "Get the kids some ice cream."

"I will, thanks." His contribution almost doubled their spending money.

It didn't take long before the children were excitedly telling other bus passengers they could see the sea. The weather was just right. Warm enough for Natalie to stretch out on a towel and read her book whenever she wasn't required to admire the network of castles her children and husband were building, but not so hot that they needed more than a good layer of sunscreen and a hat each to keep them safe.

For lunch they bought fresh fruit and cheeses from a market, a carton of milk, and bread from a local bakery, all of which they ate back on the beach. They stayed out all day, returning only to drop off their beach gear and put on warmer clothes before going out in search of somewhere inexpensive for their evening meal. OK, so you could get burgers and chips anywhere, but that's what the children wanted and as they were getting tired it seemed a wise option to feed them and get them tucked into bed as soon as possible. They picked up a bottle of cava on the way back to toast the success of their first day.

During the rest of the fortnight they spent several more days on the beach, they explored the area visiting play parks and museums and tried food from as many different local establishments as they could. Often that meant eating take aways from the containers, but the kids loved that and as Natalie didn't have to cook or wash up she was happy too. They were practically forced out of their accommodation every morning due to the noise of the workmen and there was sand from the beach and dust from the building work everywhere, but they were small inconveniences really.

Two weeks on, the family were lightly tanned and fully relaxed, her brother had his postcard and thanks to enjoying a staycation in their own house rather than a foreign holiday, Natalie and Stuart had a nicely refurbished kitchen.

4. A Lesson To Remember

By halfway through morning assembly, Adam had almost forgotten rushing to school. He often forgot things and sometimes that got him into trouble.

"Mum, I've just remembered, my tyre was soft yesterday," he'd said at breakfast.

"Did you pump it up?"

"No, I forgot."

"You'd better do it now. Hurry or you'll be late," Mum had said as she helped him with his green and yellow school tie.

Adam had pumped up his tyre as quickly as he could. He'd cycled extra fast all the way from home, across the park, past the burger bar, behind the church and into the school yard. He only just got to assembly on time.

At his first lesson, he listened to his teacher, Mr Kenzie, explaining about angles on a triangle. All triangles had three angles; he knew that already. Mr Kenzie explained how the angles could be different sizes and if they were, the triangles had different names, like isosceles and scalene. If the angles were all the same the triangle was equilateral; Adam could remember that one because the name meant equal and everything on the triangle was equal too. The other names were really hard and he had to concentrate.

Halfway through the lesson, Adam needed to measure the angles of a triangle drawn by Mr Kenzie. Adam reached into the bottom of his school bag, searching for the protractor he'd forgotten to put back in his pencil case. He felt his bicycle lock. Oh no! He'd been in such a hurry that morning, he forgot to chain his bike to the cycle rack.

Adam didn't know what to do; he couldn't interrupt his teacher and ask to leave the lesson, not without a very good reason. He wasn't sure if being forgetful was a good enough reason. The best thing, he decided, was to wait for class to finish, then instead of joining his friends for break, he would run to the cycle shed and lock his bike up. That's if it was still there. He really, really hoped it would be.

It was difficult to concentrate on the lesson after that. He kept thinking about the possibility of losing his lovely new bike. He remembered the last time he couldn't concentrate in his maths lesson. He'd been much happier then. He'd just learnt about division and was excited because he'd thought of a way to get the bike he really wanted.

Last term, he'd hoped his parents would give him a new bike for his birthday. He'd shown a picture of it to his older brother.

Kevin had said, "I don't know, Adam; it costs a lot of money. Dad's just had to get another car and I'm not sure they can afford it."

"I'd forgotten about that, Kevin. You're right, Dad said the new car was expensive," Adam agreed.

Granddad told him that if people wanted things then they had to save up the money to buy them. Adam knew about adding up and that if he put his pocket money into his building society account every week, the money would keep going up and up until he could buy his bicycle. That seemed like a good idea, except that Adam needed all his money to buy sweets and stickers. There was the fifty pence a week his grandparents gave him. He thought he could spare that.

Granddad helped him work out how long it would take to save up. First, he found out the price of the bike, £134. Then he doubled it, because fifty pence is half of a pound. It would take two hundred and sixty eight weeks. Granddad told him that as there are fifty-two weeks in a year, this worked out at more than five years. Adam would nearly have left school by then. He couldn't wait that long, so needed to find another way.

In his next maths lesson, he learnt about division, which is a way of sharing something out. Adam knew that even if his parents didn't have lots of money, they would still give him a birthday present. His grandparents and uncles and aunts always bought him something too. Even his brother, Kevin, used some of his pocket money on a small gift. Adam thought that if his whole family divided the cost of the bike between them, there might be enough money. Some people would pay more than others and Adam didn't know how to do division as complicated as that, but he guessed Granddad would know. He could hardly wait until after tea, so he could go and ask him.

After Adam explained how much he wanted a new bike and that if he had one he would be able to ride it to school, he told Granddad how he'd maybe found a way to get it.

Granddad had thought for a while. "I think that's a good idea, Adam. Me and your granny can't afford to buy you a new bike, but we'd like to help you get one."

"Do you think Mum and Dad will agree?"

"They might do. It would save your mum having to drive you to school. Tell you what, lad, we'll go round and tell them all about it shall we?"

"Yes please, Granddad," Adam said.

Just as he'd promised, Granddad explained Adam's

scheme to Mum and Dad.

Adam's dad thought about the idea for quite a while. "It's still a lot of money Adam, are you sure you really need a new bike?"

"Yes, Dad. My old one is quite small now and if I had a proper one with gears and lights, I could cycle to school. Mum wouldn't have to drive me then, when Kevin goes to senior school," Adam explained.

"That would be a help," Mum had said.

When he remembered Granddad had made that suggestion, Adam was glad he had such a clever granddad.

"I'll tell you what," Dad said. "You prove you can look after it properly and can ride safely on the roads and we'll think about it."

Granddad had winked at him. Adam hoped this meant he would get his new bike.

Granddad taught him how to mend punctures, oil the chain and change the batteries in the lights. Their local community police officer, PC Marks, offered to help make sure Adam could ride safely on the road.

"I can't have my deputy coming to any harm can I?"

The policeman called Adam 'deputy' because Adam often helped PC Marks in carrying out his duty. One time, Adam had actually arrested a really nasty burglar who pretended to be Santa Claus and had stolen lots of presents – but that's another story.

PC Marks had watched Adam cycle along the street. First very slowly and then at normal speed. Adam gave hand signals when he wanted to turn and was taught what to do at crossings and junctions. PC Marks even made him practise stopping in an emergency. After quite a lot of attempts,

Adam could do all these things properly. When he was ready, PC Marks told Dad that Adam was a good cyclist.

When Adam had come downstairs on his birthday, his brand new bicycle was waiting for him. It was red and shiny. It had lots of gears and looked very, very fast. Adam had promised to look after the bike properly, just like Granddad taught him. He promised to ride it very carefully, just like PC Marks had instructed.

Adam did always ride carefully, even when he went very fast because he was late, he still always checked at junctions and did the proper arm signals. He almost always looked after it properly too. The first time he hadn't was last night, when he forgot to pump up the tyre that was a bit flat. The second time had been just that morning when he forgot to lock it up.

As soon as the maths class was over, Adam, carrying his cycle lock, ran to the bike shed. He could hardly believe what he saw. His bike was gone.

Adam didn't run to his next lesson, he walked very slowly. He kept stopping to blow his nose and wipe his eyes. Adam thought about his lovely new bike. He'd always ridden just as PC Marks taught him and always wore his cycle helmet. Every week he oiled the chain, checked the lights and brakes and cleaned his bike. Every time Adam left his bike anywhere, he locked it. Every time, until today.

Granddad would be very disappointed with him. PC Marks will have another crime to investigate and he already had enough work without Adam causing more. Mum will probably be cross and give him enough chores to last the rest of his life, just to keep him out of trouble.

The caretaker was waiting in the classroom.

"You don't look very happy, Adam," he said. "Did you

forget to do something this morning?"

Adam nodded.

The caretaker pointed to the lock Adam was still holding. "You'd better give me that then and I'll chain your bike up for you."

"But, sir, it's gone."

"Your bike is in my office, I put it there for safekeeping."

Adam knew he would never, ever, forget to lock it again.

5. Love Of Money

Mike squinted at his wife, wishing she was more understanding of his complex personality and his needs. When he noticed her frown at him, he shielded his eyes as though the low winter sun was making it difficult to read the paper.

Angie picked up the plate which had held his breakfast – just one piece of bacon, no sausage, too many tomatoes and mushrooms, and everything grilled except the egg. "What's up with you?" she demanded.

Either he'd overdone the acting, or she'd picked up on his nervous anticipation.

"Nothing, dear," he said as airily as possible. Getting up to adjust the curtain gave him an escape from his wife's searching gaze as well as an opportunity to look for the postman. He thought he saw a flash of red in the distance. Was it just wishful thinking? He had to get that letter or he might as well say goodbye to his wife and therefore the inheritance. All those lovely gold sovereigns which each year, since he was aged about seven, he'd been permitted to pile up into stacks, trickle through his fingers and dream of one day owning. That dream was close to becoming a reality – and even closer to being snatched away for good if he didn't manage to intercept the post. Also at stake was his reputation. If the contents of that letter were made public he'd be a laughing stock down the golf club and humiliated at work.

He'd told Angie about the inheritance of course, it was pointless trying to keep something like that from her. She knew almost everything about him – a fact that was immensely comforting or impossibly frustrating depending on the situation. Every birthday and Christmas, her gift to him had helped him build up his own modest collection of sovereigns. She didn't make much fuss when he popped into the bank to open the safe deposit box and count and polish his golden beauties instead of traipsing round the shops with her, but she was less tolerant when it came to his admiration of female curves and golden hair. A lot less tolerant. Of late she always seemed to know when working late, a drink with friends, or evening round of golf meant something else.

Angie didn't know everything though. She had little idea of how many coins there'd be in the legacy left to Mike, what they were worth, nor how to collect that wonderful haul. Mike told her quite truthfully he didn't know. He had a pretty shrewd idea of the value of many of the rarer coins, as his cousin had informed him whenever he acquired one of particular interest, but Mike hadn't passed this information on to Angie. There was another secret though, of far higher importance.

He glanced out the window again, to see if the postman was approaching with the evidence.

Angie placed another log on the already blazing fire. "Mike, what on earth are you staring at? The neighbours will think you're peculiar."

"Oh, I er, have a bit of a headache."

She hurried over to him and placed a cool hand on his forehead. "Oh, poor thing. Shall I get you anything for it?"

"No, thank you, darling. I think maybe I should go for a walk."

"Good idea," Angie said, for once making no protest at his attempt to slip away from her on business of his own.

This was going to be easy. Why had he worried?

"Shall I come with you?" Angie asked.

Not quite so easy. "No, no. Don't you go getting cold."

"You're so thoughtful. Mike. Oh, I've just remembered, we need more milk. Perhaps you could get that while you're out?"

It sounded such a reasonable request. He'd have been happy to oblige if the shop hadn't been in the opposite direction from where the postman would approach. Another glance out the window revealed the red he'd seen wasn't the postman after all. If Mike left now, he could time his return to coincide with the arrival of the post and collect that letter without arousing Angie's suspicion.

Had she suggested he fetch milk on purpose he wondered as he hurried out. It was almost as though she could read his mind, the way she stopped him giving in to temptations these days. Mike had often given in to temptation in the past. He didn't entirely regret that, but he did regret leaving evidence of the last time he'd indulged in the womanly, rather than metallic, form of his desire. The temptations he'd given in to were offered by Candice 'Bubbles' Lamore. The evidence he'd left were a letter to her and a photo of the two of them featuring Mike wearing nothing but his old school tie. Fortunately it was just those two, easily destroyed, items. He was an old-fashioned sort and didn't believe in seduction by text message and email, thank goodness.

When Mike's cousin, Sir Edmund Etherington-Adaire fell seriously ill, Mike had realised that, as his closest relative and in some ways a kindred spirit, he was certain to inherit. He'd swiftly dumped Candice and spent his free time sucking up to the old boy. He'd worn the school tie again and allowed his aged cousin to reminisce about his days at the alma mater, which had been dull for Mike to listen to. He'd spent hours discussing sovereigns; their history, romance and value, which had been a genuine pleasure. And he'd gifted his cousin the very best coin in his own collection; a George III sovereign minted the year of the Battle of Waterloo, which had been painful, despite Mike's certainty he'd soon be reunited with the precious piece of metal. That had all paid off, so Mike's only worry now was that Angie would find out about the affair and force him to sell his coins in order to meet her demands for a divorce settlement. Several times he'd had to make up quick excuses when she somehow discovered he'd not been working late as he'd claimed, but he'd bluffed his way clear.

Dumping Candice hadn't been easy. He'd told her his cousin's ill health had made him re-evaluate his life. She'd been sympathetic. Too sympathetic. When the baronet died, Candice had wanted to console Mike. He'd refused in an abrupt fashion and she'd not taken it well. Too late he'd realised he now had time to resume the affair. Candice, after only a little persuasion and quite a lot of prosecco, had been willing, but admitted that in a fit of pique she'd posted the incriminating evidence to Angie. That was the letter Mike was desperate to intercept as he raced home with the carton of milk.

Yet again he was too late – the postman had visited his house. Mike dashed in, snatched the paper from his wife's hand and threw it on the fire. He knew she'd read it, but at least now she couldn't pass it on to her solicitor. His only hope was to tell the truth. Worth a go as it was the one thing he'd never tried.

He explained his affair as well as he could, being careful

to make sure she realised that Candice, drawn by his irresistible magnetism, had seduced the unwilling Mike and was now attempting to blackmail him.

Angie didn't look convinced, but waved a hand as though to say it was of no importance. "Oh, I knew about that ages ago. I've already put Candice's letter in a safe place. There's a title along with your cousin's money, did you realise?"

Unable to speak, Mike shook his head. What did titles matter? And how could Angie, who apparently otherwise understood him far too well, think it was simply the monetary value of those beautiful sovereigns which interested him?

"Yes, you're a baronet now. I don't know what that makes me, Lady something or other perhaps. Anyway, now we're going up in the world, I don't want any scandal attached to our names, which I think should be Angela and Michael from now on."

"So what did I burn?" he gasped.

She showed him the empty envelope, embossed with a solicitor's details. "The details of our inheritance. Don't worry, I did read it. I know where and when to collect the money. I think we should go together and have it paid into my account, don't you?"

Mike, sorry, Michael the Baronet, saw Candice's photo in his wife's hand and nodded helplessly.

"Don't worry, dear. If I've got the cash, title and a devoted, faithful husband I'll be quite happy for you to have all those old coins of your cousin's and for you to spend as much time as you like messing about with them."

Michael the Baronet hugged Lady Angela. She really was a wonderful, understanding wife.

6. Granddad's Cushion

One of my earliest memories is Granddad teaching me to roller skate. I wasn't scared; I had Granddad and his magic cushion. When Granddad produced that deep red square of padded velvet and his old leather belt, I knew everything would be just fine. Once he'd strapped the cushion round my skinny hips and pulled the belt as tight as one of his hugs, I was ready for anything.

I'm not so brave anymore. I haven't been brave at all in the weeks since doctors told Granddad there was nothing more they could do and allowed him to come home. He died two weeks and two days later.

I'd arranged to meet my cousin Libby, outside the church. I wasn't brave enough to get through Granddad's funeral on my own.

"There's Aunty Libby now," I told my daughter, Sophie.

Seeing Libby's tear streaked face was a shock; I hadn't realised I'd need to give support as well as receive it.

"I miss him so much, Sue," Libby whispered as she hugged me.

Knowing we were sharing the sorrow was strangely comforting. Sophie did her best to join the hug and clutched at our knees. Just for a moment I felt as confident as when I'd held Granddad's cushion and knew we'd get through the difficult few hours ahead.

"Sophie's as good as Granddad's cushion," Libby said as

though reading my mind.

"You know about that?" I'd thought it was just for me.

"He tied it around me when he taught me to skateboard and it was in the car when I took my driving test. It helped to mend my broken leg that time I fell out the apple tree and it helped mend my broken heart when my fiancé fell out of love with me. What about you?"

"Roller skating was the first time, then I had it for weeks when I was settling into Uni. I used to support my back during my pregnancy and I'm afraid I wrecked it when my waters broke!" I confessed.

"Are you two talking about the magic cushion?" asked Tina, another cousin. She told us about the times Granddad leant her the cushion to help her cope with difficult life events. "The last time was two years ago when I had all that trouble with the house."

"That can't be right. Sophie is three and the red velvet disintegrated when I washed it right after she was born," I said.

"Sue, the cushion was turquoise and shiny," Tina told us.

Libby said, "No, it was brown corduroy."

I felt betrayed. I'd long ago stopped believing in Santa and the tooth fairy, but I'd still believed in Granddad's magic cushion. Now I'd learned it wasn't something special between Granddad and me. It wasn't even just one cushion! Tears fell and even feeling Sophie's hand squeeze mine couldn't stop them. Now there was nothing at all left to help me, not even memories.

"So we each had our own magic cushion?" Libby asked.

"We must have done. It makes sense when you think about it. He had nine grandchildren altogether and I'm sure he loved us all," Tina said.

"There must have been times when more than one of us needed it," Libby added.

Would I really have felt better to know he'd helped me and not the others? I'd love the child I was now carrying with all my heart, but that wouldn't mean I'd love Sophie any less.

During his last days, Granddad held a patterned cushion close to him. Maybe the memories of his grandchildren roller skating, passing tests and carrying his great grandchild comforted him? Could it be that the magic had worked for him too? I hoped so. I looked down at my beautiful daughter and I knew that although my cushion was gone and Granddad was gone, we still had the magic.

7. Life Isn't Fair

Katy glared at the phone, wondering why she wasn't using it to call Melanie. What was wrong with a woman who couldn't phone her kid sister to congratulate her on her pregnancy? Jealousy, that's what. Katy couldn't have a baby herself, but life expected her to watch her sister experience the joy of motherhood.

"Life isn't fair," Katy had told her mum when she'd rung to pass on Melanie's news.

"I know, love," Mum said. "But remember it's not Melanie's fault. She didn't call you herself because she's worried you might be upset."

"I'll call her, once I've had time to get used to the idea."

That had been three days ago. If Katy couldn't make herself pick up the phone, she risked damaging her close relationship with her sister.

The phone rang. For a second, it seemed to her she'd made that happen. Then she saw her husband's mobile number on caller display. She answered Matthew's call.

"Katy, love. I've seen a giraffe just like yours. The lady who owns it says you can go round and talk to her about it, if you'd like to?"

Of course she wanted to do that. As well as wanting an excuse to delay her telephone conversation with her sister, she was very curious about her giraffe. Her aunt had given it to her. Their aunt had always treated Katy and Melanie the same, taking them both out and giving lavish presents. She'd loved them both equally.

At first, Katy had felt bad that she'd received the giraffe and Melanie got nothing extra. That hadn't seemed fair, but once she held the small giraffe in her hand she felt it was hers. She hadn't known why she'd got it and hadn't been able to learn much about it since, other than the fact her mum's older sister had inherited the ornament from her own aunt.

"I'm on my way." Katy slipped her giraffe into her handbag and drove off to meet the lady Matthew had told her about.

The object was surprisingly heavy and coloured black, except where the ears and feet were of burnished, golden metal. It bore no hallmarks or maker's stamp, so presumably wasn't valuable. As a child she'd liked to imagine a romantic history for it. Maybe it was made for a beautiful African princess, or had been formed from gold coins stolen by pirates, or was an ancient god. Katy never took it to a museum or jeweller in case she discovered its history was something ordinary. She had looked out for others though and learnt as much as she could about decorative antiques. That's how she'd met Matthew.

He hadn't minded they wouldn't have children. Together they'd built up an antiques business and he'd pointed out how much harder it would have been for them to attend fairs and keep the shop open if they'd had a baby to accommodate.

Matthew had hugged her tight and whispered, "Anyway, my brothers and your sister are likely to provide us with plenty of children to love."

Katy had thought she'd come to appreciate the advantages of having no children and come to terms with her disappointment until Mum had rung to tell her she was about to be an aunt.

Thankfully she arrived, at the address Matthew had given her, before she had time to get upset again. The elderly lady invited her in and made tea while Katy examined the giraffe.

"It is almost identical to mine," she said. "I'm sure they were made by the same person. Perhaps they were intended to be a pair."

The lady agreed. "I'm afraid they'll have to stay separate though. Mine is not for sale."

"That's OK, I just wanted to know what you could tell me about it," Katy assured her.

"Oh, very little. Sorry, I must have misunderstood your husband. I thought you were going to tell me ..."

Katy told the lady the little she had been able to discover. She knew what materials it was most likely made of and the probable date and country of manufacture, but nothing behind the reasons for its creation.

The lady made notes and didn't seem too disappointed. "Somehow I guessed I'd never really know very much. I'll pass on this information with the giraffe."

Katy gestured to the photos on the mantelpiece and over every wall. "Will you give it to your daughter?"

"To her, yes. She's my niece actually, I never married. It seems appropriate as it was my aunt who gave it to me."

"Your aunt?"

"Yes. Lovely lady. She used to help me build sand sculptures on the beach and take me for picnics on top of windy hills. It didn't matter what the time of year, we just wrapped up warm in winter and took an umbrella if it rained."

"Sounds like my aunt. If Mum said she thought the weather was too cold to go out, Aunty just said that's what coats were for," Katy remembered.

"I don't blame her. Time with your family, especially the children, is precious. You've got to grab it while you can, not wait for the sun to shine. That's what I've done with my niece and we've had some wonderful adventures. Well, you can see."

The lady pointed to her photos and Katy noticed they all seemed to have been taken at different locations and in every one, the girl was laughing. Katy would soon have a child to love and who she could make her laugh. Would she wait until it didn't hurt that the baby was her sister's not her own, or would she grab every chance to create happy memories?

When Katy got home she rang her sister. "Melanie, guess what? I've found out about my giraffe!"

"That's good, I hope?"

"It is. It helped me realise ..." Katy swallowed. "The giraffe thing… It means you have to make me godmother to your daughter and gives me the right to spoil her rotten, take her to the seaside and generally get all the perks of having a child without having to be the one who has to tell her off, arrange baby sitters and take her to the dentist."

"That doesn't seem quite fair," Melanie said.

"No, Sis. Life isn't fair." Katy took a deep breath. "I'm happy for you, really I am. Just give me a bit of time and soon I'll be able to show it."

8. Present For Mum

Lucy couldn't understand how things had gone so wrong. She'd wanted to get the perfect birthday gift to show her mum how much she loved her. Because she'd failed to do that the two of them weren't speaking.

She'd started thinking what to get for Mum just after her own birthday six months before. Mum and Dad had given her the kitten she'd pleaded for, even letting her select it from the animal shelter herself. How hard that had been. All of them had been so gorgeous. In the end she'd taken one which was almost adult; Frizzlee wasn't so cute so was less likely to find a home quickly. That had been Lucy's eleventh birthday, not a special one like Mum's fortieth. Lucy had to get Mum a special gift, something she'd love as much as Lucy loved Frizzlee.

She asked Dad for advice.

"Tell you what, love, why don't we go shopping together and see if we get any ideas."

Dad drove them into town and took Lucy to a jewellers. After studying the window display for just a minute, Dad went in and asked for tray E3. The jeweller brought out a tray of necklaces. Really fabulous necklaces.

Lucy stabbed her finger toward one of them. "Oh, that one, Dad! Mum would absolutely love it."

"Do you think so?"

"Oh yes! The stones in the middle of the little daisies are

exactly the same as the ones on her engagement ring and you know how she loves daisies."

"Yes, I think you're right."

Then Lucy noticed the huge numbers, which she'd assumed where something like bar codes, had little pound signs in front. Good grief, she'd nearly touched that necklace. What if she'd damaged it?

"Dad, come on let's go," she hissed, dragging him away.

"What's up, love?" Dad asked once they were outside.

She explained she'd seen the prices.

Dad had ruffled her hair. "Your Mum's worth it though, isn't she?"

"Yes, of course."

Dad couldn't have realised how expensive the necklace was. It would take years and years to afford it, even with all her pocket money, birthday and Christmas presents added together. Mum really was worth it, but Lucy needed to get her a present this year.

They did look in other shops and although Lucy saw several things she thought Mum might like, none were special enough. Not even the beautiful crystal vase with daisies engraved on it, or the lovely leather bag with a daisy motif on the flap and strap – and Lucy couldn't afford either of those.

"I'll let you have the extra money and you can do some odd jobs for me in return," Dad had offered.

Lucy had thanked him, but shaken her head. She couldn't ever do enough jobs to pay for the necklace and anyway she liked helping her dad do the garden and wash the car; it wouldn't be right for him to pay her.

· At school Lucy asked for ideas about how she could get the necklace for her mum.

"My sister won a necklace with real diamonds at the fair last year. Why not go at the weekend and try?" Sally suggested.

"Brilliant idea, thanks."

Unfortunately Lucy's parents didn't think she was old enough to go the the fair on her own and obviously she couldn't go with them if she was hoping to win Mum's present.

"OK. Can I go round to Sally's on Saturday night then, to do my homework?"

"If her parents say it's OK and you're home by nine."

Lucy set off towards Sally's house with her schoolbag over her shoulder and all her money inside it. At the end of the street she turned left toward the bus stop, not right as she would have if she'd really intended to visit her friend.

She had to buy a ticket to the fairground as her bus pass didn't cover that route. She felt uncomfortable travelling without her school friends around her. A man kept smiling at her and she worried he might get off at the same stop as her. He didn't, but there were plenty more strangers at the fair, some of them looking very strange indeed. Dad had told her she shouldn't judge people by appearances, but the men with tattoos everywhere and rings and other metal in their faces made her nervous.

It was crowded and people kept knocking into her. Underfoot it was muddy and slippery. The music was too loud and there were different songs blaring from each ride and stall. The flashing coloured lights were bright, but they left creepy dark pockets which could have contained anything. Lucy smelled grease and frying food, perfume, cigarette smoke, candyfloss and beer. She was almost ready to cry when she saw a hoopla stall decked out with watches, wads of banknotes, mobile phones and jewellery.

Right in the centre, on the tallest plinth, was a shimmering tumble of necklace. The pulsing lights from nearby rides were reflected off it, in rainbow-like beams. All she had to do was accurately throw one of the thin wooden hoops and she'd have the perfect gift for Mum. Five pounds bought Lucy a lot of hoops, but not enough. Her first few throws fell short, the next attempts overshot. The last one was the closest. She bought more. A couple of rings touched the plinth but she needed more height. By her fifth purchase of hoops Lucy's aim was much improved and almost every hoop bounced off the plinth containing the necklace, grazed against the jewels or even landed at an angle on top. She was so close to securing her prize.

Lucy's arm ached even before she'd handed over the last of her money. That last five pounds was completely wasted as her throws were worse than the ones she'd first made.

"Bad luck, love," the stallholder said. He gave her a consolation prize of a pretty bangle. It was kind of him, but no use as it wasn't nearly nice enough for a birthday present for Mum.

Lucy wandered around the fairground in search of something to eat. She was cold and fancied a portion of chips to cheer herself up. It wasn't until she rummaged in the bottom of her bag, hoping to find enough change to buy them, that the truth hit her. She'd spent every pound of the money she'd saved for Mum's present and had nothing to show for it. She gave a humourless laugh. Even if she found something cheap as chips she still couldn't afford it. Thank goodness she'd bought a return bus ticket.

It had grown dark. A glance at her watch showed she just had enough time to get home before nine; the gathering gloom was due to rain clouds. Rain fell as though someone were throwing down baths full of the stuff. Soon everyone seemed to join Lucy in attempting to leave the fairground. The full bus pulled away before she reached the stop. It left behind so many disappointed people Lucy doubted she'd get a seat on the next one either. She'd better start walking.

There was a clap of thunder and she hoped Frizzlee wasn't scared. Mum would look after her if she was, but Lucy should be there to comfort her own cat. She should really let her parents know she might be late home, but what could she say? If she claimed she was sheltering at Sally's until after the storm how could she explain arriving back soaking wet? She'd better get a move on.

It wasn't long before a car pulled up beside her. What was Dad doing out there? She ran to the car and jumped in.

"Where the hell have you been?" Not Dad: Mum.

"Sally's house ..." Maybe if she said she'd got confused in the storm she could explain being on the wrong road?

"Don't you dare lie to me! We've been worried sick. Your Dad is at home with the police. When the storm started he rang Sally's parents to say he'd pick you up and of course they hadn't seen you."

"Oh."

"Well, where were you while we were thinking you'd been run over or kidnapped?"

"At the fair." She barely whispered it.

"After what we said? Why?"

"Not telling you." How could she?

Since then the two of them hadn't spoken a word to each other. There had been plenty of talking though from Dad and the police. Lucy soon realised how stupid she'd been but it wasn't until the news on the television two nights later reported a child missing that she understood the anguish she'd put her parents through.

Dad seemed to forgive her, but not Mum. She was angry that Lucy wouldn't explain why she'd gone to the fair. Lucy could see no way to put things right. She cried in her room when she thought of Mum's birthday with no gift from her. Mum would think she didn't love her, just because she'd wanted to show she did.

"Come here, Lucy. I've got a job for you," Dad called from downstairs.

"Coming." She ran down and followed him to the garage.

"Have you been crying?"

She almost denied it. Lying hadn't done her any good, maybe the truth wouldn't make things worse. She explained why she'd gone to the fair and admitted she'd wasted all her money trying to win a necklace for Mum.

"Oh come here." Dad hugged her. "It's my fault then."

"What is, Dad?"

"I only showed you that necklace to check it was the right thing for me to buy your mum. I didn't explain as I wanted to keep it a surprise. I should have trusted you to keep it secret."

"Like you trusted me to go to Sally's?"

"Hmmm. Well I think you've learned a lesson from that." Dad showed her the necklace and the place where he was hiding it.

"She'll love it, Dad. Oh what can I give her now? It's even

more important to get her something great and I don't have any money."

"There's more to showing you care about someone than spending money."

"I suppose."

"Do you remember when you were about six you made her a papier-mâché dish?"

"Yes. Well, I don't actually remember but she keeps the ugly little thing on her bedside table, doesn't she?"

He nodded. "To her it's beautiful because you made it for her."

"Is it still there?"

"Of course it is. Just because she's angry doesn't mean she doesn't still love you."

No and it didn't stop Mum cooking her meals or washing and ironing her clothes.

"What hurts her the most is that you won't tell her why you went to the fair after we'd said no, and that you lied to us."

"I can't tell her now though, or she'll know about your necklace."

"Making up with your mum is more important than keeping her gift a secret, don't you think?"

As it happened, Lucy didn't have to say more than the first few words of explanation to Mum before she was hugged and kissed and they were both crying.

"Promise me you'll not do that again, Lucy? Even if we won't like where you're going, do tell us, or leave a note or something."

"I promise, Mum."

Every night after that, Lucy slipped out into the garage for an hour. "Just a project I'm working on," she told her mum.

Dad sometimes came out to give advice and encouragement. He helped her measure out the correct size of box to hold Mum's new necklace and to build a frame for Lucy to apply papier-mâché to. Night after night she added another thin layer. Meanwhile she had daisy flowers pressing in a book in her bedroom. When the box was completed and dried she painted it in deep blue paint, the exact shade of the sapphire eyes in the necklace daisies. Then she tweezered the pressed flowers into place and added a stone from her consolation prize bangle to the centre of each. These were sealed in place with coat after coat of varnish. The final touch was a lining of deep blue velvet.

Lucy knew Mum would love the box just because she'd made it for her, but she knew too that it was a beautiful gift, special enough for her wonderful mother.

9. Embracing Beige

I'd been thinking about the non existence of my love life and not properly listening to Gran, but one sentence had snapped me to attention.

"Who'd have thought I'd develop a passion for beige?" She actually sounded quite serious, but it's always difficult to tell on the phone.

"You can't mean it," I said.

"I am over eighty, love. Don't you think it's time?"

I didn't. I worried and I'd never once worried about Gran before.

Other people did. Mum worried when we lost Granddad. I'd mourned him of course. He was a wonderful man as fitted someone who'd earned Gran's love. I knew she was heartbroken and I sympathised with her pain, but once the first shock was over I didn't worry. Gran makes friends easily, she has lots of interests and a sense of purpose.

She moved into a smaller place. Not because at seventy-eight as she was then, she couldn't cope with the house and garden, but because on her own it took up too much time.

"One person can't do everything that kept us both busy. I'd rather give it up than do half a job," she said.

Gran decided to travel. There were so many places she hadn't seen. We went to Thailand together. The whole family rented a cottage in Italy one summer. She went with my brother to Japan and with Uncle Roger to New Zealand. She also took trips on her own. Not all alone I don't mean – properly organised tours in groups of other single people or with clubs who shared one of her interests. Gran was adventurous, not reckless.

It was on her returns from these trips that her new neighbours occasionally grew concerned about Gran. They were a friendly bunch and held each others' keys and phone numbers for family in case we needed to be contacted. We had several calls; she was out on her roof, or up a tree or otherwise doing something apparently alarming. She hadn't really been on the roof, but stood on a stool under the skylight to get a view of the carnival passing in the next street. She really did climb the tree but she'd had to in order to get down a kite. Its young owner had tried, but his small legs meant he couldn't climb as well as Gran and his short arms meant even if he had got up there he'd not have been able to reach it. Gran's always helped people.

She used to be a police woman. From the TV you'd get the idea that WPCs only filed reports and fingernails back then, but that's not true. Gran and her colleagues went out on patrols and helped in arrests, especially in cases where women or children were involved. They took statements and fingerprints. She even got to ride an official police motor scooter for a time. They were expected to behave and look ladylike though. All the WPCs had to wear quite long skirts and buttoned up blouses, covered by jackets.

"It was because of that uniform I became so colourful," she told me. "Imagine all those young women all dressed the same. I had to stand out to attract the likes of your granddad."

There must have been lots of other men interested in her, in fact I know there were as she told me about 'dear friends' who took her dancing or to the pictures but she never seemed to have noticed them much.

They were a perfect match. Granddad was sensible you see. Not that she wasn't, but he was solid, grounded. Sounds a typical man of his generation, doesn't he, but in a way he was as unconventional as her. It was he who cooked and cleaned their house. If a button came off it was Granddad who sewed it back on. Gran did work in the house. She wallpapered, re-plastered, plumbed in the shower. She went grocery shopping, but if Granddad didn't make a list she'd forget things such as bread and teabags and come back with exotic fruit they'd never tasted, or something she thought might be fish but wasn't sure and just bought because it was on offer. It would generally be Granddad's task to turn her purchases into an appetising meal.

So when she told me she was ready to embrace beige, I was truly worried. So much so that I dropped everything to go and see her. OK, I'll admit I didn't have much in the way of a social life to drop and I was owed time off work anyway, but I'd still have gone even if it had been awkward.

Gran was as brightly dressed as usual, but I didn't find that reassuring. Maybe her sight was failing?

After her usual hug I followed her into the kitchen. It was filled with cakes. Not a huge selection in brightly coloured boxes as though she were organising a tea party, but every single one a plain sponge sandwich and no packaging in sight.

"Where did all these come from?" Was it some bizarre form of kleptomania? Had she kidnapped a whole chapter of the WI and forced them to bake for her?

"I made them!"

"You baked, Gran? You?"

"Yes, I thought it was about time I gave it a go. That Mary Berry has made it fashionable and I don't want to get left behind. I did tell you it was time I gave it a go. Weren't you listening?"

"Clearly not. I thought you said you were getting into beige."

"So I did. Each cake has to be exactly the right colour on top. Not too light, not too dark but the perfect delicate beige right the way across and definitely no soggy bottom!"

I inspected the cakes. "You've nailed it, Gran. They're perfect! There are quite a lot though."

"Yes, enough for a rugby team. Go and make yourself look ravishing while I put in the jam and cream. They'll be here soon."

"You've invited a rugby team for tea?"

Of course she had. Granddad had been a rugby man and I was single. Maybe one day too I'll embrace beige, but not yet. Duncan, the scrum half, and I are far too busy to have time to bake.

10. Please Help Me!

"Helen, I need your help!"

"It'll have to wait, Debbie; I'm busy," Helen said and switched off her phone.

For a moment she felt good about that; it was time her sister learned she couldn't expect Helen to come running the second she had a problem. It was probably only something silly about the home improvements she was having done. Then, almost instantly, Helen regretted snapping. It wasn't Debbie's fault that once again she'd called at an inconvenient time. She couldn't have known Helen had been in the shower and that by the time she answered the phone she'd have shampoo in her eyes and be shivering with cold. Four-thirty on a gloomy November afternoon was no time to stand around with wet hair and bare feet Helen thought, resuming her shower.

As the water warmed her, Helen remembered the morning she'd driven like a maniac, wearing only dressing gown and slippers, to Debbie's house because her sister had rung; sobbing, "He's dead, he's dead." Helen's heart had pounded as she'd driven, fearing the worst had happened to Debbie's husband or one of her boys. It had been Harry the goldfish.

Then there had been the 'horrible accident' with the car. Helen had abandoned the wonderful cake she'd been baking and rushed into town, expecting to help with shock, insurance claims and transport home. Debbie had spilt milkshake over the upholstery.

Just last week Helen had been summonsed to deal with another disaster; Debbie's boys had a terrible illness. By the time Helen arrived, Debbie had already discovered they'd been playing with the paint roller she'd been using. The boys had tried to wash off the pale green paint but only succeeded in spreading it over their faces and hands. They did look sick; it was easy to see why their mum had worried, so Helen hadn't resented missing her favourite TV programme. Not really.

The worst timing ever had been when Debbie had called about a sporting injury just as Helen's boyfriend had taken her hand and gone down on one knee. Actually, on that occasion Debbie had broken her arm. What if there really was something serious wrong now?

Helen pulled on her now cold and wet dressing gown and called her sister. No reply. Maybe Debbie had been out somewhere when she called? Helen rang her sister's mobile. No reply. Helen called her sister's landline again. Still no reply.

She ran upstairs and dressed hurriedly; pulling on boots, without stopping to struggle into socks, and piling her wet hair under a woolly hat. Pausing only to grab her mobile, Helen drove to her sister's house. She stuck pretty much to the speed limit. Debbie's crisis probably wasn't serious, but even if it was, it wouldn't help if Helen got stopped for speeding.

Helen parked outside her sister's house and rushed up the front path. There were no lights on. Typical! Helen had rushed over for nothing. Whatever had been wrong, if there ever was anything, was obviously now sorted and Debbie had gone out. Odd that the security light hadn't come on, though. Helen continued more slowly, picking her way over broken glass. What on earth was going on?

The front door was propped drunkenly in the doorway, the frosted glass smashed. Someone must have broken in. Had Debbie called the police? Helen switched on her phone and saw she had a text from Debbie.

'Please help he's here now.'

No! Somebody had broken in and burgled Debbie – perhaps worse. Helen had been relaxing under a hot shower whilst her sister was fighting for her life. She'd been more worried about getting a speeding fine than saving Debbie.

Debbie's text hadn't been sent that long ago, perhaps it wasn't too late. The burglar could well be inside; perhaps threatening her. If Helen called the police he'd hear and might hurt Debbie. Helen crept around the side of the house to the back door. It was locked; no intruder had left that way. Helen had the key. Getting locked out had been one of the previous crises suffered by her sister.

Picking up a heavy garden ornament to defend herself, Helen eased open the door, slipped inside and tiptoed through the ground floor; no Helen. A large hammer lay on the hallway floor. Did that mean the attacker had gone?

"Debbie?" Helen whispered.

No response.

As she listened in the darkness, Helen remembered all the times she'd called Debbie for help and Debbie had rushed straight to her aid. Perhaps on those occasions Debbie had been busy doing something else which she'd abandoned to help her sister.

Helen tried again more loudly. "Debbie?"

Still no response.

Debbie had never let her down. She'd never been too busy

to help, even when Helen's problem had been a money spider in the bath or lumpy gravy when her future mother-in-law was due for lunch.

"Debbie?" Helen shouted.

There was a muffled reply. Helen raced towards the stairs. She heard footsteps on the path. Hoping it was the police, she continued.

"I've brought help," a deep voice called. "You won't be struggling now!"

Helen heard a crash below her as she reached the top of the stairs.

"In here," Debbie croaked.

Helen pushed open the spare room door and saw her sister on the floor. She'd been bound and something horrific had been done to her mouth. There wasn't time for Helen to help her; the men had reached the room. Moving protectively in front of her sister, Helen raised the garden gnome, ready to strike.

"That gnome's not going to be much help," the biggest man said.

"Don't you mess with me." Helen tried to sound brave.

"Hey, don't worry, love," he said. "We're window fitters, not double-glazing salesmen. If you don't want new windows, that's fine."

In a muffled voice Debbie said, "Put down that gnome, Helen, and tell me what's wrong."

"I thought you'd been burgled and beaten up ..." Helen trailed off as she realised that Debbie's mouth only looked odd because she was holding plastic curtain hooks between her teeth. She wasn't helplessly bound on the floor; she was sitting with curtains on her lap.

"Could you please explain why you called me and what happened after that?" Helen asked.

"I rang because Mr Plante called me," Debbie said, indicating the big man. "I'd forgotten it was today he was coming to replace the windows. That put me into a panic. When he said he'd need everything out the way, I got it into my head I had to take out the old windows. I rang you for help."

"I was in the shower... Never mind, go on."

"Ah! Anyway, I decided I'd start with the front door because that seemed easy."

"When we arrived, she'd managed to smash the door and damage the security light, blowing the lighting circuit," Mr Plante said. "We've been off getting a replacement light, fuses and our spare set of steps so Debbie here can get the curtains down."

"Which is all they really wanted me to do," Debbie said. "Why is your hair wet?"

"I told you I was in the shower."

"Why on earth didn't you dry it before you came to help me?"

"Because you're my sister. I'll always come straight over whenever you need help."

11. Famous Names

Edna Montgomery and her family had lived on Downing Street, in fact Edna still did. Although not at number ten and not in London, the address pleased Edna by being similar to the more famous version.

She'd wanted the best for her kids, so she'd named them Norma Jean and Jamie Lee. She'd bought a scrap book and pasted in the announcements of their birth which appeared in the local paper. Over the years she added more local press cuttings and photos.

"You can change it if you like, love," she'd said when a young Jamie first realised he was named after Ms Curtis. He hadn't needed to as no one other than Mum connected his name with the actress.

Jamie had wondered if Mum hoped he'd change it for something that would one day be in lights, or on the cover of a book, but it was enough for him that it was spelt correctly on his name badge at work. She'd been delighted when his photograph appeared in a national magazine and hadn't been the slightest bit disappointed when he'd pointed out it was just the company newsletter. Maybe she hadn't heard his quiet explanation as she cut out the article and stuck it in her scrap book or maybe she was proud of her family even without them becoming famous.

Jamie researched the family history in the hope they might be related to Field Marshall Montgomery as he was sure Mum would love to have a famous military hero in the family, or any other kind of famous person. He discovered one ancestor had been the doctor who opened, and first practiced, at the Montgomery clinic in town. Mum had been very impressed and added a photograph of the clinic to her scrap book.

"Coincidence about the name though. Do you think he chose the building because of it?"

"No, Mum. It wasn't called Montgomery Clinic before he worked there."

"Of course not, it wouldn't have been a clinic without a doctor."

People said his mum misunderstood things, but they were wrong about that. She understood. She just did it in a different way to other people.

"What does it mean by 'fly-drive', Jamie. Surely passengers don't drive the plane?" Mum asked one day after Jamie brought round a selection of travel brochures and suggested she do something special for her fiftieth birthday.

Jamie explained about hire cars.

"I wouldn't like to drive abroad," Mum said and picked up another brochure. "Oh look, dear. Celebrity Cruises. I'd love to do that."

"Go on a cruise, Mum? I'm not sure it's your sort of thing."

"Not the cruise bit, no, but I'd like to do a celebrity holiday. Just imagine sitting down to dinner with someone off the telly or who'd been in the paper. Do you think they do other sorts of holidays apart from cruises? I'm not sure I'd want to go to sea."

Jamie laughed, "You've done it again, Mum. Celebrity is the name of the company, not the type of holiday. I'm sure they do great cruises, but you're probably just as likely to meet someone famous on a coach tour to the Lake District."

"Really? I've always fancied going to the Lake District." She looked at Jamie's thoughtful face. "That is the pretty place with nice scenery and lots of lakes?"

"Yes, Mum, it is. I was just looking at this brochure, is that the kind of thing you'd like?"

"Ooh yes. Look at that nice friendly driver on the front and the lovely places they go to."

"In that case, I think you can have your holiday. None of us ever know what to get you for your birthday. How about if we all clubbed together to pay for your ticket?"

Edna's tour got off to a great start. The coach driver who collected her for the first part of her journey from the end of her road was the same one who had been featured on the brochure. Jamie, who'd carried her cases to the bus stop, grinned at her reaction.

"Oooh, Jamie just look at that. I'm being collected by the most famous coach driver in the world! What do you think of that?"

Jamie thought it was well worth the phone call he'd made to the coach company.

Edna sent back postcards every day, reporting both on the comfortable accommodation, delightful scenery and on her celebrity spotting.

Weather is lovely and it's going to stay nice – I've been told that by the lady who does weather reports for hospital radio in Portsmouth!

Great food and conversation every night. The couple opposite me at dinner are the Mayor of Newbury and his wife! He's often had his picture in the paper there, his wife said.

Edna phoned Jamie quite late one evening.

"I've just found out that Suzie Walters, the lady I've been sitting next to on the coach all this time, has had her picture in three different magazines. Once when she won a supermarket dash, once when she wrote in a tip about hanging washing to dry on clothes hangers so it didn't need so much ironing. I've seen my neighbour do that, just wait till I tell her I met the person who invented it! And the third time when she met Alan Titchmarsh! Can you believe that?"

"Yes, Mum. Knowing you, I can."

"Well this next bit will make you smile. She's taken a picture of me and her together as she reckons I'll be famous one day and she'll be able to send it in somewhere."

"If she's right, we'll be able to put a photo of you in the scrap book."

Edna laughed before wishing Jamie good night.

The following day, Norma came round for a chat.

"I've had a postcard from Mum. They had a tour today to a farm where they breed pigs and make sausages that were once featured on a TV cookery programme. She ate three different ones for her tea!"

"Sounds like she's having a great time."

"Yes, I just hope she doesn't realise these people aren't really celebrities and get disappointed."

"You know Mum, she isn't likely to do that."

"True."

Another postcard revealed that her current coach driver had once appeared on X Factor. He'd not got past the first round, but he could still put 'as seen on TV' on the poster when he sang in his local pub.

Bet you never thought your old mum would be eating her breakfast with a famous rock singer, did you? she wrote.

Jamie arranged to meet Norma in the pub on the evening before Edna was due home.

They were making arrangements to be at the house and make sure there was fresh milk and bread ready for her return when an announcement on the TV caught their attention.

"Now we go live to the Lake District, where the Prime Minister has been talking to locals and holiday makers."

"Good grief, will you look at that?" Norma said, pointing at the screen. "It's Mum."

Jamie asked for the sound to be turned up and everyone watched the report.

They watched, stunned, as their mum told the Prime Minister what she thought was wrong with the NHS. Several of the drinkers nodded in agreement with her words and there were shouts of, 'here here'.

"I was just saying the same to the Mayor of Newbury and writer Suzie Walters and the singer Bob Matchum the other day. They all agree with me. Now you make sure you look into it," Mum instructed the Prime Minister.

The audience in the pub cheered and then approached Jamie and Norma.

"Didn't know you had a famous mum."

"Talks a lot of sense, does Edna."

Jamie and Norma raced to their own homes to record the late news and call other relations so they too could watch it.

When Jamie met Mum off the coach he said he'd seen her

on the news and was honoured to be carrying the bags of a celebrity. "I've made a recording for you, and Norma's managed to get a picture from the report that you can put in your scrap book."

"Don't overdo it, love. I was just doing a survey," Edna said.

12. Just Following The Rules

Deena practically had to drag her younger sister down the pub. "You've survived your first week at work, so you have to celebrate."

"Celebrate isn't the right word," Kate said, after taking a gulp of her drink.

"Oh dear. I get the impression you're not enjoying it much."

"Correct." She swallowed another mouthful of strawberry flavoured cider.

"Well, shelf stacking was always going to be a bit dull, but at least it's a job and there will be chances of promotion."

"Oh, it's not the work. I quite like making the shelves look neat and tidy and sometimes I get to chat to customers and show them where things are."

"What's the problem, then?" Deena asked.

"My supervisor is Christina Greene. Remember her?"

Deena did. She'd been a prefect and often had to report Christina for being late, smoking in the toilets, or picking on smaller children. As a result Christina had jeered at Deena, calling her a snitch, teacher's pet or worse. She'd 'accidentally' trodden on her toe, elbowed her in the ribs, or knocked her with a backpack every chance she got. In games she'd send balls flying directly at Deena and tackle her over-enthusiastically. She'd threatened to do something similar to little Kate if Deena made a fuss. "Yes, she was a bully."

"She still is."

Deena remembered the time Christina had taken her school tie.

"If I'm not in uniform, I'll get detention and I know you'd want me to follow the rules," Christina had said, grabbing the end. Deena feared that if she'd not swiftly undone it, she'd have been choked. Christina never returned it and Deena had bought a new one with her pocket money rather than worry her mum about the bullying.

Deena had worked hard to pass her exams. As a result, she had a job which suited her liking for order and sticking to rules. Kate too had done her best. Christina on the other hand had put in minimal effort. "It doesn't seem fair. She broke all the rules at school and was always in trouble, yet she's still got a decent job."

"Actually, she's only acting supervisor and her attitude's so bad, I'm not sure she'll keep the job for long," Kate said.

"What does she do wrong?"

"She doesn't explain anything properly, so I get into trouble. She gave me a right lecture about stock rotation in front of the manager as though I hadn't bothered doing it, but that was the first time she'd said what I was supposed to do. Then the other day she misled me about the break times. I'm sure it was deliberate, but she just smirked and said 'rules are rules' and reported me for taking longer than I was supposed to." Between gulps of cider, Kate listed the ways Christina had mistreated her.

"Sometimes I almost regret never abusing my power when I was made prefect, I could have caused her grief then. I wish we had the chance to get our own back on her now."

Kate said, "I do a bit. Christina keeps asking after my

clever sister and saying I must be big disappointment to our family for just being a shelf stacker. I got fed up and bragged about your important job, but wouldn't say what it was. Thought I'd let her guess. She's so jealous of you she'll make up something better than I would have done."

"Jealous?" Deena asked. It didn't seem possible.

"Yes. I think she wants to do well, but won't risk trying in case she fails."

"Makes sense. A lot of bullies are insecure." She finished her drink.

"Fancy another?"

"Sure, we're not driving."

By the time Kate returned from the bar, Deena had a plan. "If she's upsetting you with her supervision, I'll do the same to her."

Deena borrowed a clipboard from work and after changing out of her usual work clothes into a smart suit, went into the supermarket in her lunch break. She walked slowly up and down the aisles with a disappointed expression, pausing to make marks on her clipboard every few steps. She made sure Christina saw her, but didn't get close enough for her to speak.

A few days later, Deena did the same thing again. That time, she walked twice past Christina. She shook her head and marked a bold cross on the chart she'd attached to the clipboard.

Christina hurried after her. "Deena? Can I help you with anything?"

"No, I really don't think you can." Deena had to rush away before she giggled.

That night, Kate said, "It's working really well. Christina

is being much nicer now. She's training me to work on the tills and explains things properly so I can do what I'm supposed to."

Deena repeated her clipboard trick again a fortnight later, just so Christina didn't start to slip back into her bad habits.

"Thanks, Sis," Kate said. "I don't think you need do it again. Christina really does seem to have changed. She works much harder too, not leaving everything to me."

"That's great news." If Christina really was a changed woman, Kate wouldn't need to fear bullying again. "Let's hope she's learned her lesson."

Over the next few weeks, Kate confirmed Christina's change of attitude seemed to be permanent. "She even apologised for not being very helpful when I started. Said she'd had things on her mind. My guess is she worried other people would do the job better than her and take her place."

A month later, Deena returned to the supermarket, simply to do her grocery shopping. She always picked times when Kate had told her Christina wouldn't be at work. She didn't want to scare the woman now she'd stopped with the bullying. She took longer than she'd intended though and bumped into Christina in the car park.

"Deena, wait!" Christina called after her.

Deena stopped. It was stupid, but she felt almost as nervous as she used to when Christina had called the same thing outside the school gates. She took a deep breath. "Yes?"

"I wanted to thank you."

"I don't know what you mean," Deena said.

"I was made employee of the month for being so good at training people. I know you must have put in a good word for me about that."

"How could I? I never saw you train anyone."

That was true and now Christina would think Kate had put in the good word and continue to be nice to her.

"Oh, no I suppose not. But it was for hard work and other things too."

"I didn't say anything that wasn't true." Actually she hadn't said anything at all, but didn't feel she need admit that. "You earned that award yourself."

Christina glowed. "It's so lovely of you to say that. Especially as I was always so mean to you at school. I was jealous and... well, thank you."

"If you really want to thank me, there's something you can do."

"Name it," Christina said.

"Promise not to bully anyone again. It's a horrible thing to do."

"I promise."

Deena left the supermarket to get back to her real job as a traffic warden. She was always as lenient as possible and didn't follow the rules to the letter. As long as the person incorrectly parked wasn't causing a danger and didn't make a habit of it, she often turned a blind eye. For a minute she was tempted to make a note of the car Christina drove and apply the rules a little more rigidly in her case, but she'd made it a rule never to abuse her position and she wasn't going to break it.

13. You're Not My Mum

Ali pouted. "It's not fair. Everyone else at school wears shoes like this."

"No they don't, Alison, and even if they did that wouldn't make me change my mind. You're twelve, not eighteen. Four inch heels are bad for your feet and totally unsuitable for school," Sandra said.

Ali stomped out the shoe shop and into the clothing store next door. She was clanging hangers together on a rack of skirts when Sandra caught up with her.

Sandra sighed. Yet again she was having to play the evil stepmother. Why couldn't she be the one who got to take Ali on madcap adventures when she should be at school? Or let her have her hair highlighted, even though her dad said no? Or buy her ridiculously expensive treats and have someone else pick up the bill? Why couldn't she just disappear whenever there was trouble, or Ali had to stick to the rules. Rules about school uniform skirts ending no more than an inch above the knee, for example.

"Not those. They're far too short," she said.

Ali threw a skirt on the shop floor. "I hate you. You're not my mum."

"No, I'm not. If I was, I'd be sunning myself on the beach with my latest boyfriend, not trudging round a shopping centre to get your school uniform."

As soon as she'd spoken, Sandra regretted it. Ali was upset

enough that her mum seemed to have abandoned her. She didn't need it thrown in her face. Perhaps it was just as well that Ali had run off after the first angry words.

Sandra picked up the discarded skirt and returned it to its rack before following Ali. It was a delaying tactic, although Sandra didn't suppose any amount of delay would give her time to think of something to say that would make things right.

Truth was, she'd never liked Mark's first wife. She was pretty and lively and perfectly charming when she choose to be, but Beverley hadn't taken to the responsibilities of marriage and motherhood. She'd often sulked or left her family and went off to find fun and excitement elsewhere. As Mark's PA, Sandra had mopped his tears and helped care for Alison. Ali liked her then, but when Mark had enough of his wife's behaviour and filed for divorce Beverley hurt everyone she could including, at times, her daughter.

Ali blamed Sandra for her parents' divorce. That wasn't fair, but she understood why the girl might think it was. Mark and Sandra had married quickly and quietly, hoping to bring stability to Ali's life. That had failed miserably, just as Sandra was now failing to locate the child.

It took a few minutes to realise the noise and panic weren't just inside her head. The shopping centre's fire alarm was sounding. People rushed by, sweeping Sandra along with them. She turned back, fighting against the tide.

"Ali!" she screamed, though it didn't seem possible anyone could hear. Where was she? Stuck in a lift, or trampled underfoot in the rush to escape, or had she hidden and got trapped somewhere. Poor kid must be terrified.

Sandra battled her way back to the shop where she'd last seen Ali. A member of the security staff blocked the entry.

She tried shoving him aside.

"That way, please, madam. Everyone must leave the building." He pointed toward the exit.

"My daughter's in there." Sandra pushed against him, yelling for Ali.

The man blocked her way. "No. Everyone is out, I promise."

He was probably right. Ali had stormed out that shop before the alarms had sounded. Where would she have gone? Sandra didn't like the idea of her wandering about town on her own, but that would be a lot better than getting trapped in a burning building, or crushed in the panic of people escaping.

"Please, madam, come with me. There's a meeting point set up for people who've got separated."

Reluctantly Sandra followed him. He ushered her into the car park where family members were being reunited. The man asked for a description of Alison and was soon contacting colleagues on his radio.

"I think we may have found her," he said after what seemed like hours but was probably only a few minutes.

Sandra followed him until he pointed to a girl talking to a police woman.

"That's her. Thank you."

Sandra rushed up, then stopped as she heard Ali sob, "She hates me. Mum abandoned me, but I never thought Sandra would. Nobody wants me."

"Ali," Sandra tried to say, but only a choked whisper escaped. She wanted to let Alison know how much she was loved and wanted by herself, Mark and probably her mother too in her own slightly selfish way.

The policewoman said, "No, Alison. I've been getting messages on the radio about your mother searching for you. She was in such a panic she whacked a security guard who wouldn't let her back into the building."

"Really?" Ali asked.

For a moment, Sandra thought Beverley must have somehow heard about the fire and returned, then she realised she was the distraught mother.

"That doesn't sound as though she's abandoned you, or that she doesn't care," the police woman said.

"No, I suppose not." Ali blew her nose.

"Want to talk? I've got a daughter about your age, so maybe I can help."

"Sandra wouldn't let me have the school uniform I wanted." Ali mumbled the words, as though already unsure she'd been right to get so angry.

"You mean she insisted you had something that actually looked a bit like the uniform and not the latest fashions?"

Ali giggled. "You really do have a daughter my age."

"Yes I do. I know how hard it is not to give in to your demands and instead to do what's best for you."

Ali nodded. "Can you call on your radio and tell her where to find me?"

"I don't think I need to." She pointed over Ali's shoulder. "Is that your mum there?"

Alison threw herself at Sandra.

Sandra hugged her tight.

"Sorry, Sandra. You must be fed up with me."

"I'm fed up with shopping for things neither of us really want to buy," she said. Anything further she might have said was drowned out by an announcement that there appeared to be no fire and the shopping centre would re-open as soon as the fire officer had declared it safe.

Ali said, "So we've just got to hang about until I can get my uniform? I won't mess about this time, I promise."

Sandra believed her, but waiting would be boring and the shopping still wouldn't be any fun even with Ali's cooperation. Why should Sandra have to do it? As Ali had said, she wasn't the girl's mother.

Someone would have to buy Ali's school uniform of course, and that someone would almost certainly be Sandra, but there were several days of the holiday left so it didn't have to be done today.

"Oh, I don't think that would be responsible of me at all. You've had a nasty shock and I think you need some sugar and a sit down. Let's go eat the biggest ice cream sundaes we can find, then go to the pictures."

"Yay! Great idea." She linked her arm through Sandra's. "You know, Mum never eats ice cream with me in case it makes her fat."

"Well she's missing out on something good." That something was the company of her daughter, but Sandra didn't say so. Maybe she was getting the hang of this stepmother thing at last.

14. A Man Called Derek

Kim used her shoulder to wedge the phone against her ear. She leafed through a magazine as she chatted to her mum. A recipe for chicken curry caught her attention. It looked good and Trevor enjoyed spicy food, but she didn't have all the required spices. If she put in the wrong ones, it might be too hot to eat, or too bland, or perhaps just plain odd. Were green cardamon seeds really much different from black ones and which kind did she have anyway? As far as she could remember the husky pods were sort of green, the individual seeds black, and the orange label didn't specify either way. If she were more like her mum, who was an imaginative cook, Kim would just adapt the recipe. Kim wasn't, so Trevor would get chicken stew for dinner. She knew where she was with a stew.

"… him at seven."

Kim dropped the magazine and sat up straight. "Sorry, Mum, what did you say?"

"We're meeting at seven, so I'd best go and see if I can do something with my hair. Speak to you later, Kim."

"Who is he?" It was too late though, Mum had hung up.

Kim replaced the receiver.

"All right?" Trevor asked.

"Mum says she's going for a drink with a man called Derek."

"That's nice."

"Nice? She's sixty-seven."

Trevor nodded. "That's plenty old enough to drink."

She gave him a look.

"You've been worried about her being on her own," Trevor pointed out.

"Yes, but I don't want her carrying on with some man she met on the internet!"

"Is that what she's doing?"

"I wasn't really listening when she first mentioned him, but it's something to do with computers."

"Don't worry, your mum isn't an idiot. I'm sure she'll take sensible precautions, such as meeting him in a public place and arranging her own transport home ..."

"That's not the point."

"What is?"

Kim didn't really know. She'd heard of people being taken in by fake bankers and the like. This man probably wasn't one of those. They didn't usually meet their victims for drinks, did they? Anyway, it was hard to imagine Mum getting caught out by a scam. Although she looked for the best in people she wasn't gullible.

When she rang Mum a few days later, she asked about Derek. She'd intended to be tactful, but ended up blurting out questions.

"Don't worry, Kim. He's not a punk rocker, doesn't ride a motorcycle and won't keep me out too late," Mum said with a chuckle before changing the subject.

Later, Kim told her husband, "I think I'm right to be concerned. He's only seven years older than me."

"That doesn't make him a bad person," Trevor unhelpfully

pointed out.

Kim rang her mother almost every day. Almost every time, Derek was mentioned. "Derek says... Derek thinks... Going to lunch with Derek."

"She's going out to lunch with him!" Kim informed Trevor.

"That's nice."

"Nice? It's Sunday lunch. She always cooked Sunday lunch for Dad. It doesn't seem right."

"I know, love." He hugged her. "Maybe she doesn't like cooking Sunday lunch just for herself?"

"No, I suppose she doesn't. I hadn't really thought about that."

Kim used to think of her parents as one unit, then she thought of Mum's grief and the practicalities of organising a funeral, notifying the bank and sorting out pension arrangements. She hadn't properly thought of Mum as a separate person, with quite a bit of life still to live.

Trevor had a business meeting close to where Mum lived and arranged to visit her. "I can't very well ask about her boyfriend," he told Kim, "but I can see she's OK."

When he returned, he said Mum was well. "And I met Derek. Nice man."

"Nice? What was he doing there? Has he moved in now?"

"He was helping set up her computer so she can talk to us on Skype. That's his job, computer tutor. We had a chat and he gave me some useful tips."

"What's he like?"

"Nice chap."

Trevor liked everyone, so that wasn't particularly helpful.

"What does he look like?"

"You know, sort of average."

"Average? You can do better than that."

"Quite tall."

At five foot four, Trevor tended to think nearly everyone was tall, so that didn't help either.

"Oh, he's got a moustache."

Kim didn't find that reassuring somehow, but it was good to hear that Mum looked well, was happy and the fridge was stocked with food.

Mum spoke about Derek often, but the news was never anything more alarming than lunch together or a trip out to buy a proper chair to sit at her new computer. She was certainly happier than she'd been in a long time and that's what was really important.

It was hard to say if it was the new man or the new machine that should take most credit for the change. Mum didn't just use the computer to chat to Kim and Trevor via Skype, she did her shopping with it and emailed relations all over the world. She looked up recipes, sent photographs and was forever finding film clips of animals in hilarious situations.

When Mum stopped mentioning Derek, Kim missed him, or at least hearing about him.

"Mum, how's Derek?" she eventually asked.

"Fine, I imagine. I've had a couple of emails, but I expect he's pretty busy at the moment."

"What happened? Why aren't you going out with him anymore?"

"Kim, I never was! I'm not sure I'll ever get involved with

another man, but if I do it certainly won't be a married one. Why would you think that?"

"Well, I ...I didn't know he was married."

"I told you how I met him, didn't I? It was a computer workshop at college. He taught there and had to stay until the end of term, even though he and his wife have bought a place in Spain and she's working out there. Sally's a teacher too, giving private English lessons. He was lonely and liked having me cook for him in exchange for extra computer tuition. Derek and I were never more than friends."

"Oh, I see." Kim confessed she hadn't been paying attention when Derek was first mentioned. She guessed Mum had been teasing her a little by not correcting her assumptions, but let that go, as she probably deserved it.

"So what were you thinking about when I told you that?" Mum asked.

"Chicken curry."

Mum laughed. "Ah! Much more exciting than me."

"It's not that and actually I was thinking of you, just not listening. The recipe needed spices I didn't have and I knew you'd have just adapted it. I'm not very good at that."

"You tell me what you do have and I'll find you a recipe. I've joined this brilliant website and ..."

Kim could hear Mum tapping away on her keyboard as she spoke.

"It's OK, Mum. I saved the recipe and bought everything I needed. There is something you could look up for me though."

"What's that?" The tapping of keys continued.

"Dating sites. There are some good ones, I understand. As

long as you meet in a public place and drive yourself, you should be fine. You might find someone nice and find your dating days are all ahead of you."

The tapping stopped.

"What did you say?"

"Trevor will be back at seven, so I'd better go and see what I can do with that chicken. Speak to you later, Mum." Kim hung up before Mum could reply.

15. Tension

Liam listened to the clock ticking. Surely it wasn't usually so loud? He moved away from it and nearer to his wife. "I didn't mean to do it," he said.

Kerry paused her knitting and glanced up at him. "Do what?" she asked.

"Whatever it is that's got you so annoyed with me." He must sound just like his father.

She pushed her glossy red hair behind her ears and sort of smiled. "I'm not annoyed."

"Good." He thought she meant it, but there was something about her. It was as though she were holding her breath.

She continued to knit but even he could see the stitches were too tight. It looked as though she were making lace. Maybe that was it, she was just concentrating on mastering her new hobby? He opened the sports pages, but didn't read. Their fifth wedding anniversary was next week, he hadn't missed that, or her birthday.

"Would you like a cup of tea?" he asked.

"Yes. I'll make it, shall I?"

"It's OK. I'll do it." He folded his paper.

She pushed the needles into the ball of wool. "I will," she insisted and left the room.

He followed her out. Watched as she dropped bags into mugs and poured over the boiling water. Good he'd get nice hot tea, not cold stewed stuff like his mother always made.

"You're not using the teapot? The one Mum gave us?" he asked.

"No." She fished out the bags and added milk.

He waited.

"Look, I know it might seem lazy to do it this way, but we only ever have one cup each so making a potful is a waste. Then it sits stewing on the side to be tipped out before we make the next one. It looks horrible, that scummy tea and the stains it leaves. Yesterday morning when I went to clean it out the smell made me feel sick."

"OK." Again he waited. There would probably be more. Mum had upset Kerry he knew and it hadn't just been her criticism of how she made the tea. They both wanted the same thing and both were repeatedly disappointed. They hadn't spoken for a while.

"I broke it," she said. "The teapot your mum gave us."

"Oh."

"I didn't mean to."

"Of course you didn't." She wouldn't. Kerry wasn't spiteful. There was something though, something she wasn't saying. He tried not to mind his tea was going to be just as cold as if she'd used the heavy pot.

"I was washing it and the smell was awful. I didn't just feel sick, I really was."

"You didn't say you were ill."

"I'm not. I looked at the calendar to check the date. That's not the only thing I checked. My hands were shaking when I saw the result. I probably shouldn't have gone straight back to the washing up, but I did and I dropped the teapot."

"It doesn't matter. I love you. It doesn't change that.

Nothing changes that." He wasn't talking about the teapot.

"It does matter though, doesn't it?"

He gave the only answer he could. "I love you." It mattered, of course it mattered, but it wouldn't help to say it. Anyway, what he'd said was true, it would never stop him loving her.

"I love you too."

He hugged her tight. No tears came. It seemed she was OK.

She said something. He must have misheard.

She said it again. "It went blue."

"But that means ..."

"It's right, isn't it?" She clutched at him. "Tell me it's right. I couldn't bear it to be wrong. I did it properly, I know I did and I was sick and I feel ..."

There were tears now. His. "Yes, I think it must be right. We'll see the doctor to be sure, but yes." He felt her relax. Almost collapse. Felt his own tension ease. He held her for a long time.

"Your mum was right."

"Oh?"

"About me being a bad wife." She grinned. "I promised you a cup of tea and then let it go cold."

"I expect you'll find a way to make it up to me."

"Probably. You make fresh tea while I try and think of something."

He did as he was asked.

"Do you think Mum will be annoyed, about the teapot?" Kerry asked.

"Do you?"

"No. I think she'll be pleased. She'll be able to buy us another one, even more awful. She won't like how I feed our baby, or hold him, or the type of nappies I use, or the colour we decorate his room, but I think she's going to be very, very happy."

16. Barbara's Legacy

The solicitor's letter, inviting me to come in and discuss matters relating to the late Miss Watkins, came as a surprise. I knew all too well there was nothing left of Barbara's business. In her last months I'd negotiated with the landowner to allow her to keep the tenancy long enough for her to find good homes for her horses. She'd done that, sometimes sending me to pose as a potential customer or member of staff to check them out first. The sale price was of less concern to her than the way the animal would be treated.

"I don't want to die in debt, but I'll do it rather than letting them down."

"Of course." I'd only known her just over two years, but that she cared more for her horses than anything else was obvious from the start.

"I've made a will. You'll get anything that's left, but if it's so much as a lead rope you plaited yourself, you'll be lucky."

She was right in that there was nothing worth any money remaining by the time she'd paid what she owed and breathed her last. I was moved though that she'd left me her books and photos. That meant nearly as much to me as the trust she'd shown in listening to my opinion about who would be permitted to buy her beloved horses.

I did briefly wonder if there might be an insurance policy or investment somewhere which had got overlooked, but soon dismissed the idea. Barbara was organised, with every scrap of paperwork neatly filed. Besides, if she'd had money for those things, she'd have spent it on the horses. I went anyway though. I'd left school two months before and hadn't yet found a job despite trying hard. Throughout my last term I'd applied to almost everywhere which had anything directly to do with horses. Then, after my exams, I'd applied to anywhere indirectly connected with horses; feed merchants, saddlers and even a supplier of riding clothes. Recently I'd widened my search and applied for any job I thought I stood a chance of getting. No interviews conflicted with any of the dates the solicitor had suggested, so I agreed to the first of those.

The solicitor, who so far I'd only spoken to by telephone, introduced himself and then quickly explained his role as executor of Barbara's estate, confirmed I'd received the few items which made up my inheritance and provided papers for me to sign. There was also a cheque for £3.47. Not even as much as the bus fare I'd have paid to come and collect it, had I decided against cycling.

"There's one other thing ..." the solicitor said.

"Yes?"

"Miss Watkins left certain, er instructions."

Of course she did. If Barbara had any last words for me they wouldn't be gentle platitudes or even suggestions, but definite orders regarding something she wanted me to do.

"She would like you to go here and speak to Mr Granger." He passed me a slip of paper with the address on.

I didn't need to read it. Charles Granger had once been a world class show jumper and now owned a prosperous stables where he bred and trained horses. He'd have been top of the list of places I'd applied for a job had it not been for George, the horse he'd bought from Barbara. George was her best, most loved and most valuable horse. When she sold him we both cried. It was then that I realised it was true; Barbara was dying and my time with her and her horses would soon be over. I guessed her tears were for the same reason, minus the part about me of course.

There had been no need for me to go and check out Mr Granger's establishment before the sale was agreed, so the only time I'd met him was when he collected George. Barbara had by then been too weak to lead him up the lorry's steep ramp and I was so upset I couldn't even do up the head collar. Mr Granger had taken it from me, swiftly fitted it and led George away. Neither of them had so much as glanced at me.

"Miss Sandall?"

"Sorry, what did you say?"

"Would you like me to ring and arrange an appointment?" the solicitor asked.

I nodded. What choice did I have? This was one of Barbara's orders and maybe I'd get to see George again. I felt I was almost ready for that.

"Would this afternoon be convenient?" I was asked, after the solicitor had explained why he was calling.

The stables were sort of on my way home, I had nothing better to do and putting it off would have made me nervous.

Mr Granger shook my hand half an hour later, showed me where I could leave my bike and offered tea.

"How did you get interested in horses, Martha?" he asked once I'd taken a few sips and eaten a chocolate biscuit.

I didn't know why Barbara had wanted me to meet him or what she might have said and had no idea if he remembered me. He did seem genuinely interested though.

"I think I was probably born that way. I can't remember a time when I didn't love them. All my dreams and ambitions growing up involved horses. They varied a bit. I was going to be a princess riding around in a crystal carriage pulled by unicorns at one point. Other times I was going to be a show jumper like you, or win races. You know the kind of thing."

It seemed he did as he smiled and offered another biscuit before encouraging me to continue. I decided to give him the whole story.

I don't know if I have selective memory, or there really were a lot of horses in my childhood. My grandparents took me for a proper seaside holiday which involved pony rides on the beach. A cousin was driven to her wedding in a horse and carriage. Two of my school friends were pony mad for a while. Their parents paid for them to have riding lessons once a week and they worked in the stables sometimes. I went too whenever I could, just to be with the ponies. Mum couldn't afford lessons for me and I usually had to save my pocket money to pay to get the bus over there.

The people at the stables were lovely and always thanked me for my help mucking out, poop picking in the fields or clearing them of weeds, and I spent hours grooming the animals. Just being close to the ponies would have been reward enough, but I was given a few short lessons.

I wasn't jealous of the other two that their parents could afford lessons and drove them everywhere, but I was furious when they decided the stables stuff was just too much like hard work. It broke nails and took up time they could be hanging about looking for boys.

I decided to try to get a part time job at a place nearer to me. Not a riding school, but a private yard I knew very little about. I wouldn't mind if it was unpaid as long as I could be near the horses and perhaps ride occasionally. It was still a three mile journey, but there was a cycle path so I told Mum I was going for a ride. No job had been advertised, but I knew where horses were involved there was always work to do and the lady who ran the place apparently worked alone, so I was very hopeful she'd take me on.

The first time I met her, Barbara yelled at me.

"What are you doing here?'"

Somehow I stammered out that I wanted a job.

"No jobs here and I wouldn't employ a silly little kid like you if there was."

I tried to tell her I knew how to muck out and she wouldn't have to pay me if I could ride her horses, but when I answered her question about where I'd learned to ride she laughed so hard she had trouble breathing.

When eventually she got herself under control she told me to clear off. I cycled home, furious. Didn't tell Mum about it though. I'd intended to tell her when I had the job all sorted out. She's hot on not letting people down so I'd have persuaded her.

Perhaps Barbara had thought I really was a silly little kid, who'd be like my friends and let her down? If I could just prove that wasn't the case, maybe she'd change her mind. Took me a while to pluck up the courage to return to Barbara's, but I went back.

At first I couldn't see her in the yard, then I saw her out in a paddock with a horse. She was holding his foot, as though about to pick it out, but even to me it seemed odd she'd do it in the middle of a field and I guessed something was wrong. I didn't know if that would make it better or worse and hesitated by the gate. Soon I heard her yelling and incredibly it was for me to get over there quick. There was no doubting the urgency of her voice.

I ran. When I got closer I saw blood. It was all over her and seeping from where she held the horse's ankle.

"Come here, girl."

I did as ordered.

"Get down." She pulled me onto my knees by her side. "Put your hands by mine. When I let go you have to clamp your hands where mine are and squeeze tight. Understand?"

I thought I did, but when she removed hers and a great arc of blood spurted out, I saw I didn't have a clue. Barbara pressed my hands in place.

"Hold tight and don't let go. His artery is severed and he'll bleed to death if you do. I'm going to call the vet."

"I could do that."

"Can you get into my house, find the phone, know what number to call and what to say?"

I don't know if I answered, but it must have been obvious I couldn't. That I was just a silly little kid.

"Do not let go," she barked.

She removed the pressure of her hand. Immediately blood began to gush between my fingers. I used both hands together and pushed hard until it was just a gentle seeping.

"Be quick," I told Barbara. "I can't hold on like this for long."

She'd already gone and was running towards her cottage.

I was terrified. First that the horse would die and then that when he did he'd fall on me and crush me. This was no pony, but a huge great beast and from my position under his belly I could see he was a stallion. From the way he was standing so placidly with a strange and terrified girl gripping his leg, I assumed he must be very weak or possibly in shock. Could horses faint, I wondered. That they slept standing, I knew, but presumably unconsciousness or death would bring them down.

Naturally I was on the side with the injured leg. If I moved to the other side, instead of being crushed I'd simply run the risk of being struck by a hoof as he fell. Possibly safer for me, but with my arms outstretched I wouldn't be able to apply as much pressure, so worse for him. I stayed where I was.

It seemed a very long wait. I could no longer feel my fingers and I realised more blood was flowing under my weakening grip, but there was absolutely nothing I could do. My legs and back were in agony and tears and snot ran unchecked down my face. That beautiful creature, who was meekly and trustingly allowing me to help him, might die.

Eventually Barbara returned. She stroked the horse's muzzle and spoke softly to him. "Help's coming, George. Hold on, there's a good boy." Then she turned her attention on me. "If you let go will you get on that bike of yours and cycle off?"

I couldn't tell if that's what she wanted or not, but my concern for the horse was greater than my fear of her. "I can't just leave him."

She nodded, then knelt beside me. She put her hands ready and when I let go she applied pressure. Much less blood spurted out that time. I didn't know if it was good or bad. Had he lost so much the pressure was weaker, or had our changeover been swifter?

"Go and open the gate wide." Barbara nodded towards the paddock gate. "Then the one to the road. Wait there for the vet and bring him up here."

"OK." I did as she asked.

The vet managed to stop the bleeding. He stitched George up and gave him various injections. George was taken into a stable and given food and water. I did that, following out Barbara's snapped instructions as she continued to stroke and soothe him. I remember very little of it. Once it seemed that all which could be done had been done, I started to shake and the stable spun.

Barbara was full of thanks to the vet. It was he who pointed out I needed someone to take care of me as I seemed to be in shock.

"That's all I need," Barbara muttered.

I was put in front of a fire, wrapped in a blanket and given sweet tea until my teeth stopped chattering. I was even allowed to use her bathroom to wipe off the worst of the blood before I cycled home.

Even so, you can imagine how Mum reacted when I got in. Persuading her I was fine was hampered by the fact that really I wasn't. That had been a Sunday term time and it was winter and dark after school, so I wasn't allowed to go back until the Saturday. OK, I wasn't strictly allowed back, but Mum had no idea the experience hadn't scared me so much I'd never want to see another horse, so she hadn't banned me from returning.

I didn't exactly get a warm welcome from Barbara.

"I told you I don't want you here. It was probably stupid kids like you who set off the Chinese lanterns."

Although I couldn't really see what was wrong with that, I knew I was innocent and said so.

I learned a lantern had landed in her paddock and it was

the wire remains which had cut and nearly killed her best stallion. The 'nearly killed' reassured me he wasn't dead and I knew I'd contributed to that. I told her I at least deserved to know if he'd be OK.

"Do you now?" She stomped off towards the stables.

I followed. It was that or get on my bike and go home, never to return.

George looked fantastic and just a bit frightening. His ears pricked forward as we approached, his coat gleamed and he stamped impatiently in his stable.

"Wants to be out," Barbara said. "Want to take him for a ride?"

There was a challenge in her voice. One I wasn't stupid enough to accept.

"That probably wouldn't be a good idea."

"He's fine. A gentle walk would do him good. You'd have to keep him on a tight rein though, make sure he didn't trot and pull his stitches."

"I don't think I could do that," I admitted.

"No need to be modest, I know you've had lessons."

"And we both know I still don't have a clue."

Barbara laughed again, but nowhere near as harshly as when I'd tried to convince her I did know what I was doing. She let me feed George a couple of carrots which I managed to do without getting my fingers bitten off.

"There you go then, you've seen he's all right."

"I still want to work here. Not for money, like I said, just to be with the horses and maybe learn a bit. I'm willing to work really hard and do whatever you say."

"Are you now?"

I tried to assure her of that.

"And what do your parents think of the idea?"

"There's just my mum."

"You'd best go home and ask her, hadn't you? Come back tomorrow if she says yes."

If I'd thought convincing Barbara was hard, it was as easy as handing out sugar lumps compared with getting Mum to agree. She insisted on coming to meet Barbara and exchanging phone numbers with her and that I promise to be careful and do my homework first, be home by six at the latest...

Barbara worked me hard and I had the three mile cycle ride each way, but I loved it. I learned a lot. The first lesson was that most of the stuff I'd learned at the riding school was rubbish. They wasted a fortune on straw the way they mucked out for example. Lead ropes and hay nets weren't things to be bought, but items made from string recycled from hay bales. I learned that new jodhpurs and the kind of fancy riding jackets my friends had worn were a waste of money, but good boots were essential.

"You can't get so much work done with crushed toes or a twisted ankle," she explained. Don't think though that she bought me a pair; she lent me a set of hers and told me to wear extra socks.

My assumption that she couldn't afford to pay me although she desperately needed the help was proved to be correct. I learned you have to work hard for what you want and that it means more if you earn it. Barbara had done a job she'd hated, what it was I never did learn, but it had provided the money to set up her stables, and the pension was just about enough to keep them going.

I also learned that Barbara had a heart after all. One capable of caring a little for those on two legs despite her loving only those with four. Her horses needed more exercise than she had time to provide.

"I'm not having them messed about with so I'll have to teach you to ride." She pretended not to notice how delighted I was.

Even then I thought I already knew the basics, but fat riding school ponies hadn't prepared me for horses with spirit. They weren't vicious and were accustomed to me handling them, but they were big and wanted to do more than stand still and be petted.

Barbara started me off on an elderly mare. Although fairly docile she wasn't used to looking after beginners and she was huge. Just getting on was a challenge, but once Barbara started us trotting round in circles on the end of a long lead rope I found it was one I had to repeat several times each lesson. The mare got quite good at stepping over me and continuing her circuit.

Barbara said, "If you can't stay on, could you at least fall off somewhere which is less in the way?"

I noticed though that before I'd arrived for the first lesson, she'd spread a thick layer of her precious straw over the floor of the barn where I was to practise.

"Do you think I'm deliberately falling under her legs?" I asked when I'd got my breath back and scrambled once more to my feet.

"Looks like it from here!"

"I'm holding on as tightly as I can."

"Yes, to the reins but they won't keep you up, girl. Use your legs and your weight and your balance. Move with the horse, not off of her."

Each week I improved. George was fully recovered long before I was ready to sit on his back and be led around a paddock, but I did do that. Twice.

Barbara must have suspected she was ill long before I found her slumped in the tack room. Even then she tried to pass it off as just being a bit tired. By then I'd picked up some of her stubbornness and abrupt manner and ordered her to see a doctor.

"If you won't help yourself, I won't help you either. You can muck out and feed your own horses."

I'm not sure I meant it, but it worked and she made the appointment. The first time she spoke to me with anything of the gentleness she used for the horses was when she told me she had just months to live.

"I need to find homes for the horses. Good homes. Will you help me?"

"Of course."

I explained the steps we'd taken to Mr Granger. It wasn't until I mentioned George's departure that I remembered I was talking to his new owner.

"Can I see him?" I asked.

"Of course."

Mr Granger showed me out to a paddock. The grass was lusher than any I'd seen at Barbara's place. The fencing was far smarter and the gate shiny and new. The horse looked no better though. No amount of money would have seen him better cared for than the way she'd treated her animals.

George's coat gleamed in the sun and his ears pricked forward when I called to him. He trotted over to us.

Mr Granger handed me a head collar and lead rope. It wasn't made from recycled bale string, but I guessed being new and expensive wouldn't stop it doing the job. I climbed into the paddock, fastened the collar around his head and led George to where Mr Granger had opened the gate.

"Would you like to ride him?"

"I would, yes... but although I've learned quite a bit from Barbara, I'm not up to handling him on my own yet."

"That's OK." He waved towards the stable block and someone came running.

"Take George in will you, Brett, and get ready to give this young lady a riding lesson."

"Sure thing, boss."

As the man led George away, I asked Mr Granger, "Is that why Barbara asked me to meet you? So I could learn to ride George?"

"No. She asked... no insisted, that when I next had a staff vacancy, that I interview you."

"Oh!"

"Do you still want a job in a stables?"

"Yes! Yes, definitely. I'd absolutely love to work here. I can bring you my CV anytime. There's not much on it and I'm still waiting for my exam results but I do have some experience. Er, well you know about that now and I can come for an interview whenever you like."

"I don't think we need bother with any of that; you come very highly recommended."

"Does that mean ...? Have I ...?"

"If you're willing to start on minimum wage whilst you're being trained and happy to start straight away then yes, you've got the job."

"Thank you," I said, accepting the final part of Barbara's legacy. I'd treasure her books, the £3.47 would be useful to buy mints for George and of course I was delighted to have a job I was sure I'd love.

"And thank you, Barbara," I whispered as I made my way to the stables. "Thank you for teaching a silly little kid some valuable lessons and for caring enough about her future to ensure she'd continue to learn after you were gone."

17. Stop Fussing!

"There you go, love," Susanna's mother-in-law said as she pulled up outside the entrance to the health centre. "Now, where shall I meet you?"

"There's no need for that, I can easily get the bus back," Susanna said. She'd have preferred to get the bus in for her pre-natal check-up too, but Mum insisted she'd have driven into town anyway. She fussed so much Susanna wondered how she'd ever got through her own pregnancy.

"We could go for a coffee, love," she offered. "Shall we say The Bluebird at eleven? I'll treat you to a cake as you're eating for two now."

Susanna, gritted her teeth to prevent her pointing out the idea of eating double during pregnancy was now considered outdated. Doing that would only upset Mum and in any case, Susanna hadn't fancied much breakfast, and probably would be hungry by eleven. She gave in. "That will be lovely. I'll see you later."

In the busy waiting room, Susanna was glad she'd talked her mother-in-law out of coming in with her. The woman would have been frantic at the thought of Susanna having to stand and share the space with people who might actually be ill. Fortunately the health centre scheduled pre-natal classes and checks so that didn't actually happen.

Susanna didn't even have time to flick through a magazine before her name was called.

"What have you got planned for me today?" Susanna

asked Cassie, the midwife. "Not more tests, I hope. I'm pregnant, not ill. Why do I need all this fuss?"

In the silence that followed she realised she'd taken her irritation out on Cassie.

"Sorry ..."

The midwife smiled. "Think of it this way; has your house ever burnt down?"

"No, but ..."

"We've never had a fire here either, yet you can see we have smoke alarms."

"Yes." Susanna guessed Cassie had changed the subject in order to calm her down. It was working. They had smoke alarms at home; the two they thought they needed and the extra ones Mum had bought for them. "They're for reassurance and as an early warning system – just like these tests?"

"Exactly. You don't have to have them if you really don't want to, but I strongly recommend you do."

"Yeah, sorry."

Cassie nodded and said, "How about I check your blood pressure?"

Susanna rolled up her sleeve. "Yes, but if it's high don't panic. It'll just be because my mother-in-law drove me in."

"Oh dear, bad driver is she?" Cassie asked as she placed the cuff around Susanna's arm.

"No. It's just that she fusses about my 'delicate condition'. She had her one child very late in life and I guess she had a rough time." As she explained to Cassie, Susanna began to understand her mother-in-law's anxiety. "Things have changed a lot since then, I suppose?"

"Yes. Thankfully."

Susanna removed her dress and lay on the bed for her ultrasound. Cassie spread gel onto Susanna's belly and then moved the device firmly, but painlessly over the surface. Susanna was able to watch on the screen as Cassie pointed out the baby's head, limbs and heartbeat. Cassie also printed out the image.

"You don't want to know the sex, do you?"

"No!"

"That's fine. I won't tell you then."

Susanna had done it again. "Sorry. Steve and I don't want to know, but his mum does. She's desperate to buy loads of things in pink or blue."

"Oh, I see. She's going to spoil the baby rotten, isn't she?"

"Yes." If Susanna didn't strangle her first for interfering. She forced herself to speak cheerfully. "I'm sure I'm having a boy, but either is fine and I want that surprise to look forward to when I'm going through labour."

"Sounds fair enough to me."

It sounded reasonable to everyone, or at least everyone Susanna had explained it to.

"Thanks. I'm sorry if I was stroppy earlier. I know you're doing your best for me and I do appreciate it, honestly."

"Don't worry about it. We'll blame it on your hormones shall we?"

"Thanks, Cassie."

"No problem. Is your mother-in-law driving you home?"

"Yes, but first she's treating me to coffee and cake as I'm 'eating for two'."

Cassie grinned. "I prescribe some high quality chocolate

on that cake, to help with your iron levels."

Mum was waiting outside the health centre when Susanna came out.

"I thought I'd walk with you, or I can get the car and drive you if you prefer."

"Walking is fine." Susanna spoke as calmly as she could.

They hadn't got two steps before Mum asked, "Well, are you having a boy or a girl?"

Susanna explained that she didn't know and why she didn't want to.

"Oh, yes, I see. I suppose you're a bit nervous about having the baby."

"A bit, yes and to be honest ..." She lost her nerve before she could explain.

"What is it? Is something wrong?"

"Not with the baby," Susanna quickly reassured her.

"With you?"

"No. I'm afraid it's you. You keep fussing over me and it's really annoying."

They walked on without speaking for a while. Then Mum said, "I'm sorry. I don't really mean to interfere, it's just this will be my first grandchild and I'm excited. I know it's your baby not mine." She looked like she might cry.

Susanna squeezed her arm. "My child, your grandchild. Let's make a deal – you stop fussing over me and save up all that attention for the little one."

"OK, I'll try to contain myself until he, or she, is born."

"There's no need to wait so long. I have a picture from the scan. To thank you for driving me in today, I'll treat you to that coffee and cake while you drool over the baby."

18. Doing The Right Thing

Veronica switched on the TV and sank onto the sofa. She reached for her cup of tea, ready to enjoy the last instalment of the drama she'd been following. The phone rang. She tried to ignore it, ten to one is was a salesman wanting to sell her windows. The ringing continued. Maybe it was important. Veronica muted the television and answered.

"Hello, Aunt Veronica, I just wanted to thank you for sorting out all that trouble with Malcolm."

"There's no need, I didn't do anything really." She hadn't; just listened. True, she'd given up the nice day out she'd had planned in order to listen to various members of her family, whine, complain and try to canvass support until they'd calmed down enough to talk to each other, but perhaps Kelly, the neighbour who'd issued the invitation, would invite her out again another day.

"Oh you did, there'd have been a real family crisis without you," her niece insisted.

Veronica was treated to a recap of the entire story. It was good to hear the problem had been resolved and everyone was happy again, Veronica just wished she could hear about it at another time. Still, it wouldn't be right to cut short the call just to watch a TV programme.

"You always do the right thing," her niece finished by saying, just as the credits rolled.

In the kitchen, Veronica poured away her cold tea and reboiled the kettle. She reached for the biscuit tin, but put it back in the cupboard unopened. It would soon be time for supper and she didn't want to spoil her appetite. A proper meal of salad and tinned fish would be much better for her than a handful of chocolate cookies, however delicious they might be. She poured milk into her tea, then almost dropped the carton as she heard a squeal of breaks, followed by an unpleasant crunching sound. She raced outside.

A young lad was sprawled in front of the car. Veronica hoped he wasn't as badly hurt as his bike which was scrunched up under the car's wheel. The driver was out the car, trying to lift the boy.

"Don't touch him," Veronica yelled. "Don't move him until we know what's wrong," she said more gently as she got closer.

"I didn't see him, he came from nowhere." The man was pale and shaking.

"Do you have a phone?" Veronica asked. She told the man to call for an ambulance and gave him the address. Then she knelt by the boy, bending her head to assure him, "Help is on the way."

He seemed not to hear, but at least Veronica could see his chest rise and fall.

As people came out of neighbouring houses, Veronica asked them to direct traffic around the accident, to fetch blankets for the boy, and the driver, and to try to find the boy's parents.

The boy opened his eyes and tried to sit up. "What happened, is my bike OK?"

"Please, just lie still," Veronica soothed.

A paramedic arrived on a motorcycle and examined the boy. "Think he'll be fine, but you did the right thing by not moving him."

The ambulance and a police car arrived together. The boy was taken to hospital for checks and the driver questioned. Veronica's sensible response was praised. The interested crowd began to melt away.

"Come in for a cup of tea," her neighbour offered.

Remembering her second cup, now cold, in the kitchen Veronica accepted. "Thank you, I could do with it."

As she made tea, Kelly added to the praise Veronica had already received. "You always do the right thing."

"Yes and I'm fed up with it!"

"Oh."

"Sorry, I didn't mean to snap. I expect the accident unsettled me."

"I expect so. Now sit down, drink your tea and, if you like, you can tell me all about it."

"Oh, there's nothing to tell really."

Kelly shrugged, fetched a plate of cakes and sipped her tea. The scent of cinnamon wafted up from the plate and the cakes glistened with honey drizzled over the top.

Without meaning to, Veronica began to talk. She explained to Kelly, that as a child she'd always been a good girl. She'd been the oldest daughter, so cared for her siblings. As a teenager, an attractive bad boy had shown interest in her, but Veronica was sensible and not tempted. Or at least, she hadn't given in to the temptation.

Veronica stopped talking then and absentmindedly ate one of the small sticky cakes. Kelly prompted her to continue.

She'd taken a safe, sensible job in the civil service, she said, and now had a reasonable pension, but couldn't help wondering what would have happened if she'd followed her totally foolish dream of becoming an artist. She had a nice, practical house to live in all paid for, but no happy memories of blowing her wages on wild holidays.

"Well, do something wild and silly now," Kelly suggested.

"Oh, I couldn't. I wouldn't know how." Without meaning to, Veronica took another cake and lifted it to her mouth.

"I don't think you really want to – that's why you never have. Bet you couldn't do anything but the right thing, however hard you tried."

Veronica finished the morsel of cake and licked her fingers. "Is that so? Well, eating the last of your cakes wouldn't be the right thing, would it?"

Kelly pushed the plate towards Veronica, as though daring her to do it.

Veronica hesitated. "Oh well, perhaps you're right," she admitted as she pushed the plate back.

Kelly laughed. "Told you! Don't feel bad though. You possibly saved that boy's life today by ensuring people did the right thing and you've made it easier for the police to learn what happened. That might prevent further accidents."

"I don't think …" Kelly was being dramatic. All she'd done was make sure nobody did anything reckless.

"And from what I gather, you stopped a major family row by delaying our trip to the gardens."

That probably was true and it was good to hear the trip was postponed, not cancelled. Veronica smiled and gestured towards the last cake. "Do you have a knife? We could have half each."

"Now that's definitely the right thing to do!"

19. Albert's Soup

Albert's friends came to dinner. They hadn't been invited.

"Can't have you moping," one of them had rung to say. "We promised Albert we'd look after you, so we'll be round on Wednesday for dinner. Don't bother with wine, beer will do us."

Marie, used to doing what was expected, didn't have the presence of mind to refuse this generous attempt to boost her morale.

She had no worries about what to feed them. It would be a Wednesday after all. The freezer was full with Albert's soup and pies. Deciding what to wear wasn't difficult either. Her black dress would be perfect. They'd all seen it recently, but wearing something bright and pretty seemed wrong.

How to behave was trickier. Devastated? Bravely carrying on as before? Making the most of the situation? No, not yet and not with them.

The men were very kind, or rather probably convinced themselves that was true. They brought her flowers; the cheapest on offer in the local shop. They fetched in, and drank, Albert's beer supply from the garage, to save her the trouble.

Marie served generous quantities of meaty broth.

"Delicious," they said as they drained their bowls.

Marie dished up the pie, with big chunks of sweet meat. They each cleared their plates. The operation was followed by another pie, this time filled with gooseberries.

One of the men cornered her in the kitchen, hinting how lonely she must be without Albert. He offered to comfort her.

She quickly returned to the others with hints of her own – that it was time they all left.

Albert's mother came to dinner the following week. She hadn't been invited either.

"Can't have people saying I'm neglecting you," she rang to say. "I'll be round on Wednesday for dinner. Try not to burn it."

Marie attempted to reply, but was talking to a dead line.

She had no worries about what to cook. There was still plenty of Albert's pies and soup in the freezer. Deciding what to wear wasn't difficult either. Her black dress didn't really need to go to the cleaners yet.

How to behave was trickier. No, actually it wasn't. She'd be wrong whatever she did, so there was little point worrying.

Her mother-in-law didn't bring flowers. She insisted Marie open a bottle of Albert's wine, but after a few sips remembered she was driving.

Marie served large portions of meaty broth.

"Did Albert make it?" his mum demanded. That woman didn't believe Marie was capable of doing anything. Although to be fair, Albert had had more than a hand in this soup.

Marie smiled sweetly and offered seconds. "Albert made a lot of soup."

"With proper meat stock, I hope?" his mum asked.

"Yes."

"Good, I don't like waste."

Gosh a word of praise, even if it was meant for her son who was no longer around to hear it.

"Neither do I," Marie said.

She didn't like excessive penny pinching either, but now wasn't the time to criticise Albert. Instead Marie described how the boiled bones were placed into a hessian sack and bashed with a lump hammer and the results put on the garden as bonemeal to feed the roses.

Marie dished up the pie, with big chunks of sweet meat. Albert made a lot of pie too. One for every Wednesday for the next three months. And enough mince for every Thursday, a roast every Sunday. Thanks to Albert she still had a diet as regimented and boring as the one he'd always insisted on. It seemed she'd never eat anything else for the rest of her life.

"It's so odd his going off just like that," his mum said. "And with a friend I've never met."

That part was indeed a little odd, Marie couldn't help agreeing. Not that Albert should disappear without her, but it was odd his mother had never met his friend. There wasn't much anyone could keep secret from that woman.

Marie described John as best as she could. "He's average height. Not quite so much meat on him as Albert. Brownish hair."

"Could be anyone."

"Custard with your rhubarb tart?" Marie asked.

Albert's mother left as soon as she'd eaten. Marie received no offers, welcome or otherwise, to ease her loneliness.

Albert and Marie's daughter came to dinner. She didn't need to be invited. Caroline was always welcome.

Marie dressed in the pretty top Caroline had given her last birthday, selecting her brightest skirt to match. She hugged her daughter and made no attempt to hide her delight at seeing her.

"I'm sorry I couldn't come before, Mum. I feel bad that it's been three weeks since I said goodbye to Dad."

"You're here now, love. That's what matters."

No Albert soup and pie for Caroline. That wouldn't be right. Instead they worked together to cook up a light, fluffy omelette. They followed it with strawberries and cream and shared a bottle of wine which Marie had bought specially.

"It's so odd without Dad here," Caroline said.

"Not having a go at you for refusing to eat dead creatures you mean?"

"Well, yes."

"Or having a fit for buying expensive fruit out of season when there's half a freezer full of mushy rhubarb and sour gooseberries from his garden?"

"Well …"

"And as for the wine!"

"Mum, I …"

"It's all right love, I don't expect you to say anything disloyal, but to you I can't pretend I'm missing him."

"Not at all?"

"I hardly get a chance. His mother and friends have been checking up on me and there's the freezer," she shuddered. "Er… and I've got a job."

"A job! Wow that's fantastic." Caroline hugged her mum.

"It's just cleaning in offices a few hours twice a week."

"Nothing wrong with that."

"And thanks to your father I'm very good at it."

"Must be a bit different, doing it on an industrial scale."

"Oh it is. No mud and manure from the garden, no vacuum held together with sticky tape and hope, no exploded glass bottles from wine making ..."

"Mum I ..."

"Sorry, love. I shouldn't moan to you. It's not fair."

"It is. You said I shouldn't be disloyal to him but I should be loyal to you. I'm surprised you put up with it for so long."

"He was lovely once," Marie said, swallowing a lump in her throat.

"Yes, I remember him being so much nicer when I was little. What happened?"

"Your gran."

"Ah."

"He was living well away from her when we met. She wasn't exactly a ray of sunshine then and never really took to me. Your dad and I were were happy for almost ten years. Then we moved back here after your granddad died. Your gran became a horrible, unreasonable woman. She couldn't stand to see anyone happy, not even her own flesh and blood. She developed a phobia of spending money too, which she passed to your dad."

"I'm surprised you've never snapped and done something drastic to her."

"Perhaps I should have?"

"She's not worth the jail time, Mum. In fact she's not worth your time at all."

"Maybe you're right, love. I have tried to get on with her, but she's not interested."

After that Marie distanced herself from Albert's mother and his friends. She asked for her work hours to be increased. The readiness with which her supervisor agreed gave Marie's confidence a boost and the extra money improved it further as she could afford to have her hair cut, buy new clothes and a lipstick. She went to the pictures, read magazines and cooked herself a variety of different, tasty dishes.

Her mother-in-law arrived unexpectedly. Marie didn't invite her in.

"I saw you earlier, carrying shopping bags," Albert's mother almost hissed.

"And you've come to apologise for not stopping to offer me a lift?"

As her mother-in-law turned purple and gasped for breath, Marie wondered how long it had been since anyone spoke up to her. She worried the older woman would drop dead from shock on her doorstep, which would be extremely inconvenient.

"It's my own money I've been spending. I got a job," Marie explained.

"A job!"

"I know Albert wasn't keen on me getting one, but he's not here, is he?"

"What have you done with my boy?" she screeched.

Knowing that having a row on the doorstep would just draw unwanted attention, Marie brought her in. She made tea and allowed her mother-in-law to check she was keeping the house in good order.

"Where's the wedding photo which was on the mantlepiece?" Albert's mother demanded.

Resisting snapping, 'none of your business,' Marie took a deep breath and said, "In the framing shop in the High Street. The cardboard frame had got very tatty."

That was true. After their wedding they couldn't afford anything else for a while. Marie supposed they'd just got used to seeing it that way. By the time it was beginning to curl and look scruffy, Albert was back home under his mother's influence and wouldn't waste the money.

"And what are these?" She snatched up Marie's postcards.

"They're all addressed to me, but feel free to read them." The sarcasm was wasted.

"Why are there so many?"

"Five isn't many in two months."

"This doesn't sound like my boy at all!"

Was Albert's mother the only person who'd consider it totally out of character that he'd used phrases such as, 'I'm missing you'?

Eventually Marie got rid of her. To cheer herself up she invited all her new work friends round for a meal. It was a squashed but fun affair and had the added bonus of using up the last of Albert's soup and pies.

She was returning from work one day when she found two policeman waiting outside her house.

"Are you Mrs Albert Spears?"

"What's happened? Is Albert OK?"

"That's what we're here to find out, madam. May we come in?"

The policemen accepted coffee and asked a lot of

questions. The younger one indicated the newly framed wedding photo.

"Is that your husband?"

"Yes, but obviously it's not recent. I have others." Marie flicked through an album of pictures which showed Albert and her happy. It was obvious they'd become less so over the years. Albert had got fatter and fatter and Marie was melting away, almost as though he were taking over their joint space and she was becoming his shadow. In the few recent ones they both looked downright miserable.

The police wanted to know when Albert had gone and where. Puzzled, Marie provided as many details as she could."I think it was a midlife crisis or something. He made this new friend."

"John Smith?"

"Yes, that's right."

"And totally out of character decided to go to Patagonia for three months?"

"Exactly. It was quite a shock to everyone." Actually that wasn't true. Most people hadn't even known about it until he'd departed.

"John had booked it with his brother and it was all paid for, but the brother dropped out at the last minute, so it seemed too good a chance to miss. My husband loves a bargain."

"So you don't have any receipts to show he purchased these tickets?" the older policeman asked.

"I don't understand why you're asking all this. If you think something may have happened to Albert, surely you know where he is?"

"We didn't say anything had happened to your husband,

madam. Why would you think it had?"

"Because I haven't seen him for almost three months and two policeman are asking questions about him! What's happened? A plane crash or ..." She stopped herself suggesting he'd been eaten by crocodiles.

"Sorry, we didn't mean to alarm you. We're simply reacting to reports we've had. Do you mind if we look around?"

"I suppose not, but I still don't understand."

She started to though when they looked in the freezer, making notes of the contents, and poked around under the rose bushes.

"Has my mother-in-law been making allegations?"

"We're not at liberty to say," the police said.

"If you want to take samples, feel free." They wouldn't find anything, not even what her mother-in-law had presumably told them to look for. All the Albert soup and pie had been eaten. The ground up bones she'd sprinkled not in her garden, but in the park. She hadn't wanted those sharp little pieces causing her trouble later.

The police looked undecided. Were they doubting her innocence or just worried that if they broke protocol in any way they'd damage their case?

"There's one simple way to sort this out," she told them. "He's due back next week. Why not wait until then?"

Albert must have been surprised so many people were waiting for him at the airport. His friends looked quite pleased to see him. The police looked surprised. His mother seemed downright disappointed.

Caroline, who'd received a card from him just the day before pushed through them all. "Dad!" She hugged him.

Marie would have greeted Albert much less enthusiastically if she could have got near him at all. The police formally asked him who he was, checked his passport and had him confirm where he'd been. His mother said a great deal, but was so angry only the odd word could be understood. The police escorted her out.

Marie hoped wasting police time was an offence which carried a long prison sentence.

"What's that all about?" Albert asked.

"Your mother seems to have told the police I killed you," Marie said.

"Eh?" Albert asked.

"Whereas really she's just going to divorce you," Caroline told him.

"Eh?" Albert and Marie asked.

"That's what you said, Mum."

"Not exactly. What I said was I wasn't going to put up with your penny pinching, being controlled by your mother or living a boring rigid life where even our meals are planned in advance. I want some freedom and some fun."

"Of course you do," Albert said. "I knew this trip would change me and it has. I missed you so much. You too, love," he said to his daughter.

"I read the card you sent Caroline," Marie said. In it he'd apologised for the unkind way he'd treated their daughter.

"I was behaving like Mum," Albert said. "I started to realise that when I saw how different I am from John. He wrote to his wife nearly every day, even arranged for gifts to be sent back, whereas for the first week I didn't send so much as a postcard. John tried all the local food. I wasted the first few days searching out foods I was familiar with, only giving up because they were so expensive. John pointed out I'd wasted three days in paradise with grocery shopping. It brought me to my senses and I saw I'd been wasting most of my life these last few years."

"You have," Marie agreed. "Are you really going to change, or will you slip back into your old ways in a few weeks?" She meant would his mother get to him, but didn't think she could mention that woman calmly.

"I'm really going to change."

Marie was sceptical, until his mother phoned and demanded he come to see her that evening.

"Not tonight, Mum. I want to spend some time with Marie."

He refused to go the next day too as he'd probably have jet-lag. Her angry voice only stopped when he disconnected.

More postcards arrived. As the trip had gone on he'd written more frequently, sharing his exciting experiences and saying they should travel together next time he could get away from work.

The packages came soon after. A beautiful hand-woven scarf in vibrant colours, bundles of sweetly scented cinnamon bark and a box of spicy wild peppercorns, a handmade vase...

Marie and Albert invited his mother for dinner. Marie wore a new dress, with the scarf Albert had given her draped artistically around her shoulders. Candlelight glinted off their newly framed wedding photo and cast intricate shadows from the flowers in her Patagonian vase. From the kitchen wafted an appetising and spicy aroma.

"Do you think your mum really will come and eat it?"

"I don't know, love. All I know is I'm so lucky and grateful you gave me a second chance, I can only hope she'll feel the same way."

Marie had a bottle of Albert's gooseberry wine chilling in the fridge just in case.

20. Totally Unsuitable

Celia stomped downstairs to answer a knock at door. As she'd suspected it was the postman wanting her to sign for a parcel. Nothing unusual in that; the postman was just about the only person who called.

She assumed the huge box was for a neighbour, but her own name and address were printed on it. She must finally have won a prize! A hamper of luxury biscuits perhaps, or maybe it was from that competition for embroidered cushions or something nice for the garden.

It didn't take long to slice through the sticky tape, pull open the box and remove the protective packaging. Celia had won a baby gym! What could a woman in her sixties do with a baby gym? True her muscles could do with a bit of toning up to make up for hours spent tapping away on the computer, but the brightly coloured plastic equipment was far too small for her.

Celia ran her hand along the gym and wished she had a grandchild she could watch playing with it. She'd lost any chance of that three years previously when she'd fallen out with her daughter.

None of her friends and neighbours had children the right age. Maybe she could offer her prize to the people on the websites she used to track down all the competitions she entered. There was bound to be someone who had a child the right age. Probably several people and she wouldn't know who to send it to and there'd be postage costs. She'd have to think about it.

Celia smiled in anticipation of the comments she'd get when she announced she'd won a competition at last. The members of the sites she used were very supportive when she'd first joined and shared lots of tips with her. They'd be pleased at her success. Celia had hundreds of Facebook friends, twitter followers and internet buddies, yet her own family couldn't stand her. Well, it was their loss.

She packed away the gym and decided it was time to think about lunch. She'd better have couscous again; she only had to eat two more packs of the stuff and she could send away for the free place mats (not exactly a prize, but close enough).

As she ate, she flicked through her latest magazine. Celia had never bought any until she took up comping as a hobby. Now she regularly bought a dozen magazines a week and was never short of something to read. She liked the funny reader's letters and uplifting short stories best, but sometimes her attention was caught by a true life tale. Tragic some of those were. Especially those about families who fell out for silly reasons and lost contact.

Celia had been too harsh with her daughter, she saw that now. She'd been so upset when Leigh wanted to drop out of college to marry that awful musician. Celia said, "It's him or me."

Leigh had chosen the boy she'd only known a year or so over the woman who'd raised her, loved her and worried about her for all of her seventeen years. Leigh wrote later saying he, the awful boy, when told of Celia's ultimatum told Leigh to go back to her mum.

He made excuses for you. Said it was the shock of our engagement, that you don't really know him and might come round once you do. He said blood is thicker than water. That I could easily get another husband, but not another mother. That I could leave him or see him in secret; whatever I wanted. So now I know I was right to choose him, not someone unwilling to see the good in the person I love.

It took Celia some time to understand the choice Leigh had made. Too long. If only Celia could contact her daughter now, but it was far too late. Leigh had married, she was fairly sure. Celia didn't know her daughter's new name. Celia herself had moved home; the house was too big for one person, too full of painful memories, so Leigh couldn't contact her mother either, even if she wanted to.

Celia tried to pull herself together. It was no use getting worked up about the past, better to concentrate on problems she could solve. The baby gym for instance. She'd give it away to a new mum and maybe pass on a few tips too, stop someone else making the mistake she'd made.

That afternoon she got the bus into town, determined to put a card up in a shop window. The children's toy and clothing store wouldn't want to advertise something they had on sale. The off-licence didn't seem the right choice, nor the travel agents. How about the post office? That seemed the best option. It didn't take long to write out a card stating the gym was free to a good home and add her name and phone number.

She'd not been home long when the telephone rang.

"Hello," a man's voice said. "I saw a card in the post office window. Are you really giving it away?"

"Yes, but only to someone who has a child who'll use it, not to someone who'll just sell it."

"I have a baby girl who'd make good use of it. I'd be happy to bring her round to show you when I collect the gym if you agree to let us have it."

"Oh, I didn't mean ..." Celia mentally reprimanded herself. She shouldn't have implied he might be lying. Had she still not learned to look for the good in people?

The man said. "One look at her and you'll see your gym will get plenty of use and she loves travelling in the car."

"Then do please bring her." It would be lovely to see the child and imagine her playing with Celia's prize.

"Can I ask why you're giving it away? I'm sure you could have sold it."

Celia told him about her competition success and then, because he sounded genuinely interested, about her failure at motherhood.

"I'm so sorry you've lost contact with your daughter. Our Rebecca doesn't see her grandparents very often which is sad."

Celia was glad he didn't ask if she had grandchildren as she'd have had to admit she didn't know.

Celia returned to town later in the week to buy cakes. She intended to try making friends with the couple. Maybe they'd welcome that if their own parents didn't live close by?

The man knocked on Celia's door exactly on time. Sure enough he was carrying a baby. Little Rebecca was so cute, exactly how she'd imagined her own grandchild might look. The dad, Robert he informed her, was obviously a wonderful and loving father. He held the baby carefully, gently controlling her squirming attempts at escape.

"My, she is lively!" Celia said. "I see what you meant about the gym getting plenty of use." She looked behind them to where the mother stood in the doorway. Although this girl was the right age, it wasn't her daughter. Celia hadn't expected she would be, but she'd hoped.

The young family stayed to tea once they were assured Celia didn't mind little Rebecca crawling around the flat.

"She moves fast and has a habit of grabbing at anything and everything," Kerry, the young mother, said.

"Shall we try her with the gym, see if it keeps her in one place?" Celia suggested.

As soon as Rebecca was placed on a mat, so she could reach the different objects suspended above her, it was clear the baby loved her new gym. She gurgled and laughed with delight as she grabbed the fluffy red ball, pulled at the springy yellow tube and discovered pressing and squeezing the blue frame produced a variety of noises.

As they ate cake and drank tea Celia studied Kerry.

"I'm sure I've seen you somewhere before," Celia said.

"I wasn't sure you'd recognise me. I went to school with Leigh." Kerry looked embarrassed. She'd have heard Celia had fallen out with her daughter, from her husband if she hadn't known already.

"Do you still see her?" Celia asked.

"Yes."

Celia didn't want to further embarrass Kerry but she couldn't pass up the slight chance of making contact with Leigh. "Could I ask you to pass on my telephone number to her. I don't want to cause you trouble, but if you could tell her I'd like to see her?"

Kerry seemed relieved. "I could, but it would be better if you did it yourself, don't you think?"

Celia admitted she couldn't.

"Yes you can," Kerry said. "When Robert told me the

name on the card and what you said when he called, I told Leigh." She opened her handbag and pulled out a slip of paper. "Here. She asked me to give you this."

Celia recognised her daughter's handwriting on the note. She couldn't read the number for the tears in her eyes, but she knew she'd stop crying soon and would make the call once her visitors had gone. For now it was enough to know she'd won something better than anything on offer in a competition; a second chance with Leigh.

21. To You, My Darling Daughter

I was twenty-two when I first met your father. At work it was. I didn't like him much back then. He was younger than me for a start. That shouldn't have mattered, the very fact that it did probably proved I lacked his maturity. He was better than me; at lots of things, in lots of ways. I resented that. Then he left the company and went on to something better. I liked him even less then.

A few years later we met again. At a conference I hadn't wanted to attend. Can't even remember what that was about but I remember he smiled and spoke to me as though we'd been friends, as though I hadn't snubbed him time and again in the past. Had he forgotten the truth or just pretended not to remember? I must ask him sometime.

Thankfully I'd grown up enough by then to be civil and accepted his offer of dinner in the hotel that night. I accepted his next invitation too and the next. I didn't even realise I was falling in love. Can you believe that? He told me he was moving away. He was clever enough to see what I hadn't seen for myself and before my tears could flow he proposed. I still cried, but from joy.

We married soon after. The wedding was arranged so hastily that friends guessed I was pregnant. I wasn't, there simply wasn't much time to waste between your father being sure of my love and his having to leave for Africa. I did manage to spend a little time with Mum, planning, looking at flowers, tasting food for the reception. I wasn't that fussed about the details and did it mostly for her. I'm so glad now that I did.

I know how much it would mean to me to see you in your wedding dress, giggle with you as we selected the delicate underwear and clothes for your honeymoon. Tease your dad over his speech. My mum gave me 'the talk' just before the wedding. That won't be needed for you my love, just as the dress and ivory basque aren't needed.

So my wedding was small and simple, but lovely. There was no honeymoon, we went straight to our new life in the bush. You weren't conceived out there and we told ourselves that was a good thing. We thought about you though, talked about you. We loved you even then.

We moved back to England, bought a house opposite a park with swings. We made sure it was in the catchment area of a good school as well as convenient for our work and social life. We were happy but waiting. Waiting for you.

We waited a long time. A very long time.

There were signs and tests and then a little more waiting.

The wait is over now. I had a hysterectomy yesterday. I barely have the strength to hold the pen and my handwriting is all but unreadable. That doesn't matter as you'll never read this, my darling. You never were more than a wish, a hope. I loved you though, loved you so much. And, now I can't hide from myself the fact that you'll never be, I mourn. I don't mourn your loss but the loss of the hope of you.

Now I must wipe my eyes and try to look cheerful. Your father will be here soon. He'll want to ask how I am but I shan't let him. Instead I'll ask him how he felt when he saw me at that conference. Today he'll say something sweet I expect. Usually he'd tease me, but I guess he won't do it whilst I'm in a hospital bed. He'll wait until later. We've got good at waiting.

I'll get over the operation and get well again. It was successful the surgeon told me, no trace of the cancer remains. No trace of hope for a child either, but of course he didn't say that.

Soon my husband will take me home. He'll hold me tight and love me and as I grow stronger we'll have you again my love. You'll live where you've always lived, in the love between us.

22. Zombie Goldfish

"How do you fancy ten pin bowling on Saturday?" Melissa asked as casually as possible.

"Great idea, Mum," Dan said.

"Yeah, I'm up for it," Kirsty added.

Melissa briefly considered suggesting the possibility of Tom coming with them. The kids seemed to like him and would probably be happy for him to accompany them but she had to be careful. Kirsty once jokingly referred to him as 'Mum's boyfriend' and she didn't want the kids to feel she might try to replace their dad or that she wasn't putting them first. Her kids were wonderful. Without them she'd never have survived losing her dear Theo. Wouldn't have wanted to. They were everything to her.

Maybe she needed to allow them some space though? Tom had hinted as much. Perhaps she tried too hard to protect them from all hurt and had forgotten her own needs. Take that horrible goldfish for example. She'd never wanted the flipping thing even before it turned into a zombie. The kids had been enthusiastic for about a day and a half and had massively overfed it before losing interest. Amazingly it didn't die from all that food, just floated around on the top for a few days before recovering. It was Melissa who cleaned the bowl, changed the water and fed it every day for the next three years. In the weeks after Theo's accident the fish got forgotten. Visiting him and comforting the kids had been her priorities. Melissa, when she realised she'd not attended to it for over a week, dreaded finding it dead, possibly even rotting. She certainly didn't want the kids, who'd just begun to realise Daddy was never coming home, to have to see it.

She'd wandered into the living room trying to think of a quick distraction tactic should the fish be dead. Dan's rucksack had blocked the view of the bowl.

"Mum have you taken up yoga or something?" Kirsty asked.

"No, why?"

"Just wondered why you were standing in that strange position."

She couldn't lie to them. They'd had enough with well meaning people promising Theo would be OK. "Thought it was time I cleaned the fishbowl. I haven't done it lately ..."

Dan came and hugged her. "It's OK, Mum. I did it while you were at the hospital this morning."

"Oh thank you, love!"

The fish was fine. It did look a bit thinner than before, but that was hardly surprising.

Almost exactly a year after Theo's funeral, Melissa found the fish floating on the top of the bowl. Unlike when he'd been overfed he wasn't pathetically flipping his flippers. He wasn't doing anything at all. She was sure the kids would be upset, so decided to replace it.

Melissa didn't get the chance. Kirsty had an accident at school. Her teacher, Tom, knowing about Theo, didn't just phone but came in person and drove her to hospital. Kirsty wasn't badly hurt but had been knocked unconscious so had to stay in overnight, just to be safe.

Melissa phoned Dan to let him know what had happened.

"Don't worry, Mum. I'm sure Melissa will be OK and I can get the bus home."

When she got in at five he was watching the goldfish. Thirteen year old Dan was none the worse for spending an hour alone. The fish too looked fine. Well as fine as the horrible bug-eyed thing ever looked. Kirsty too made a full recovery. She stayed at home for a few days and Tom dropped in to check on her and leave her some work.

The fish didn't have another of its strange turns for over two years. By then Melissa was less concerned with her kids' reaction should it really die. She needn't have worried as it made another full recovery. By then Melissa reckoned it had to be at least six years old, assuming it was very young when Theo had bought it.

Just six months later Melissa found it floating again. It wasn't dead-looking this time but clearly not well. She rang Tom, who despite Kirsty now attending the senior school, occasionally called in for a cup of tea and a chat with Melissa.

"I think the goldfish is dying again. Please tell me the kids will cope with that."

"They'll be fine, Melissa, but what do you mean by dying again? I'm no expert but I think it's just cats which have nine lives."

"It's some kind of zombie. It keeps dying and making a full recovery," Melissa explained.

"How odd. Can I come round and take a look?"

Half an hour later they stood side by side looking at the fish. Melissa had almost plucked up the courage to mention the planned bowling trip when Dan and Kirsty came home. They pulled faces, giggled and had a very staged talk about how much they were looking forward to going bowling.

Melissa ushered them into the kitchen. "What's up with you two?"

"Are you going to invite Tom bowling with us?"

She shook her head. How could she now? She'd wanted to tactfully find out how they'd feel first and give them a chance to accept the idea of their mum having a relationship. And then there was the fish.

"Well you should, Mum," Dan said. "Four people works out better than three for teams and anyway it's time you got a life."

"Plus he obviously fancies you," Kirsty added.

The kids left her doing a pretty good impression of a dead goldfish. When she followed them they were discussing the Zombie with Tom.

"I think it really is dead now," he said.

"Staying that way this time. I don't think Mum needs us to get her another," Dan said.

"What?" Melissa squeaked.

"We knew you'd be upset when it died so we bought a new one each time," Dan explained.

"I don't know what to say."

"Then I'll do it for you," Kirsty said. "Tom would you like to come bowling with us on Saturday?"

"And then take Mum to dinner afterwards," Dan added. "We've been looking after her for years, it's time someone else had a go."

23. Keeping In Touch

"I'm worried about Mum and Dad," Richard said.

Rosie looked up from her book. "What's happened?"

"Nothing. I just wish it were easier to contact them."

"There's this marvellous device called a telephone …"

He smiled. "Why does nobody tell me these things? You know I like to keep up with modern technology."

Rosie stuck out her tongue.

"You know I phone them, but what with the time difference and me being so busy it's not easy. If they were on Facebook or mobiles so I could text it would be better."

Rosie leant over and squeezed his hand. "I suppose it's only natural to worry when they're so far away, but they seem fine to me. They've got the beach hut. Walking down there is good exercise and they enjoy it, and at home they've got their hobbies."

"Crosswords and knitting? Not exactly keeping up to date, are they?"

"I don't know. Crossword clues often involve current affairs and knitting and craftwork is getting trendy again."

"Maybe, but Mum and Dad aren living in the past. They need to meet new people, do new things."

"They did say they were thinking of doing some course at college. That'll get them mixing with new people."

"That was months ago. They might never do it."

"Family trait that, is it?" Rosie asked.

"What do you mean?"

"You keep saying we'll set up Skype on the computer so we can talk to the kids without spending a fortune on calls to Hobart and Perth."

"Yes all right, I'll do it when I've finished this report. It's nearly there."

"And then you can phone your parents and put your mind at rest."

He nodded again and continued with his work.

"OK, that's done. Now let's see about Skype," he said a short while later.

It didn't take Richard long to set up an account for them and email the boys to let them know it was done. Then Richard rang his parents.

"What's the weather been like?" he asked. It was hardly an original topic of conversation but better than nagging his parents for being behind the times.

"Lovely! Well it is for sitting on the beach. Probably not so nice for those stuck in stuffy offices."

"It is tiring, I admit," Richard said.

"You're tired because you work too much! When I was your age we didn't have modern technology to get everything done quicker, but we still had time to relax at the end of the day."

"Technology's not all bad. I've just set up Skype so Rosie and I can see the boys as well as talk to them."

"About time! What's your user name?"

"RichRose? Why?"

"So I can call you back on that and save your phone bill of

course." She hung up.

Moments later Richard's computer made a noise very like an old fashioned phone and a message appeared to let him know Knitting Nora wanted to speak to him. Richard clicked his mouse. "Mum?"

"Yes, dear, here I am. Can you see us?"

"I can." He waved to his parents who waved back.

"Hello, Rosie dear," Mum said as Rosie moved to stand behind her husband. "This is much better we can all have a proper chat. I never like to talk too much when it costs you money and it's difficult to know when to call you, what with the time difference and your long hours."

"You're right, Mum, it's much better. So tell me all about you getting a computer."

"We did that college course I mentioned. Great fun it was and we soon saw the advantages so we persuaded the neighbours' boys to help us buy and set up this computer."

"Good, right. And have you been down the beach hut lately?" He tried to return the conversation to something more usual while he adjusted to the idea of his parents now being online and easy to contact.

"Yes. We took a picture to go on our blog."

"Blog?" Richard asked.

"It's like an online diary, dear."

"I know what a blog is, Mum."

"Sorry, you seemed confused. Anyway, we're in touch with people who have all kinds of different hobbies. You might want to take a look yourself and find yourself something interesting to do. I worry about you, Richard."

Richard hoped his parents couldn't hear Rosie laughing.

24. After The Clocks Go Back

I have a reputation for poking and prying, especially in this café. A well deserved reputation, I suppose. It must seem like that's what I do. Actually, it is what I do. Although I'm barely middle-aged I give the appearance of a nosy old woman, just because I have an urge to know people's problems. Not to amuse myself, not to gloat or have something to hold over them. Never that, though I do understand why some believed it. They wanted to believe it, those whose problems I couldn't solve, or who didn't want them solved, or didn't want to share or didn't even have a problem at all, though I thought they did.

I do have a problem, I see that. I can't pass anyone who's sitting and crying. People do usually sit to cry, have you noticed that? Or maybe they're just the ones I see. With head bowed into the shadows, hands covering their face, they could be anyone. When I lightly touch their shoulder, or sit opposite and wait, they'll look up eventually. And I could see dark brown eyes, a mascara streaked face, that the hands are tipped with fuchsia pink nails. I might notice that some of the dark shadows, into which their face had withdrawn, are silky skeins of chocolate coloured hair. Straight hair, the straightness you only get after a long session with heated tongs.

That's not what I usually see though, when finally they look up at me. I see a different face. Sometimes one I know, usually one I don't. Usually they speak.

"What do you want?" is a common response. Or even, "What do you want, Amanda?" or "What do you want, now?" if it happens to be someone who knows me. What they say, how they say it doesn't matter, just as long as they give me an opening. The chance to say what I must.

Generally I'm all right then, or rather they are. Maybe it's the same thing. I try to tell myself it's the same thing.

"I want to help," I say. I always say that and it's true, I think. Yes, yes, it is true.

"You can't, no one can." That's a fairly typical reaction.

"Would you like to talk about it?" I'll reply. Or "Try me," or anything else which seems appropriate, encouraging.

"No," or "Go away," often comes next.

"OK, but I'm just here if you want me." Then I stay close by, but not too close.

Usually they don't come over, but it has happened so I always wait. I've heard people say I haunt this café, but it's not like that at all. The ghost here isn't mine.

Not everyone asks me to leave them alone. Sometimes people tell me their problem right away, or allow me to coax it from them. Sometimes just talking helps. I see it has, even if afterwards they wish they'd never told me they thought their husband was having an affair, that they can't pay the rent or about the guilty secret from their past. They think I'll tell, I suppose. I never do. I never will. Worries, guilt and skeletons in the cupboard, we all have them, don't we? Sometimes it's better to get these things out in the open, but it's not my place to do that.

A few times there's been no problem, or none I've discovered. A piece of grit in their eye, or "I've just been chopping onions. You really are a daft bat, Amanda

Higgins!"

I'm not sure about the grit, but the onions were right. That had been Sonia who owns the café now, and she'd been preparing a cottage pie. She does a good cottage pie, nearly as good as Mum's was when she and Dad ran the place.

Sonia's one of those who thinks I poke and pry, but I don't think she condemns me. Maybe the people who she took over from told her what happened right outside the café, about the time the clocks went back, thirty odd years ago. Sometimes she lays a hand gently on my arm or sits opposite me and waits, but I never ask her what she wants. She might say she wants to help and I couldn't bear that. I can't be helped, don't want to be. What I want, what I need, is to help others.

If I'm really lucky the problem is simple, easily remedied. That happens.

"I can't get home," Lucy wailed, though I didn't know her name at the time. She uttered those few words, drew in a long, sob-laden breath and released a torrent. She told me about the long term boyfriend with whom she'd split up that night. About being stranded here where she knew no one. About her stolen phone and general poverty. Then about her mum who would be sick with worry and the dad who would kill her.

We talked for quite a time. I bought her a coffee. She wiped the mascara from under her dark brown eyes. She ran fingers through hair, which I guess had been perfectly straight when she'd left home that evening, and talked some more. That's when she introduced herself as Lucy, just after I'd seen she didn't have those dark eyes, that brown hair I remember. The girl was a stranger, but one I could help.

Lucy's boyfriend hadn't been any good. She told me she'd

realised it at last and dumped him. Being no good, he'd yelled at her to get out of the car and then driven off, taking with him her bag and the phone it contained. She had seen lights ahead and walked, in shoes as tight as they were tall and pretty, to the café. But then she was stuck without a way to get home, or to contact her parents. The parents who'd be concerned for the safety of their little girl. I could imagine them; worry, anger and love combined. For a moment I imagined those emotions destroying them and all around them. Then I did as so many others did when I offered to help them; I pulled myself together.

It was nine o'clock, Lucy's parents wouldn't be frantic yet, they probably wouldn't even be concerned above the constant low level niggles about the unsuitable boyfriend.

"There's a bus stop outside and a payphone round the corner. I'll lend you the money to get home, or call your parents." I'm not sure why I said lend, not give, as I didn't expect it would be returned and in any case I didn't begrudge her the small amount.

Lucy took a handful of coins. I waited, heart thumping as she stepped outside. It was OK though, she returned after a few minutes to say, "My dad's on his way."

She did give back the change, but not the coins she'd used. As I said, I'd not expected that. Something else I didn't expect was the card which came a week later. The envelope was addressed, in the large curly letters still popular with teenage girls, 'to Amanda c/o the café'.

"This must be for you," Sonia had said and dropped it onto the table in front of me. "Open it then," she eventually demanded.

That was just after the clocks had gone back. That's always the worst time for me.

I knew then how some of my victims felt. They wanted to be left alone with their misery and there I was poking my nose in, trying to get them to let it out into the open. Trying to let it be blown away, but of course they didn't all see that.

"It'll be from that girl you helped get home safely, I bet," Sonia said.

Realising she was right I ripped open the envelope. The card was pretty; a field of wild flowers. Inside, all over the inside, was a scribbled note of thanks, from which I gathered she'd got back her handbag, phone and self respect. She'd not left much space for it, but underneath her parents had each added their thanks and neat signatures. There was also a gift voucher. Not for a huge sum of money, but easily enough to buy myself some flowers, box of chocolates or a new lipstick so I could paint on a bright smile.

Sonia was still there I realised as the tears fell. My tears. "It's nothing," I said. "I'm fine and anyway, there's nothing anyone can do."

I left the café then to buy flowers. Not for me. For her, the girl I didn't help. Didn't even try to help. I saw her, sitting with her head bowed into the shadows, hands tipped with fuchsia pink nails covering her face. A face overhung with silky skeins of chocolate coloured hair. Straight hair, the straightness you only get after a long session with heated tongs. I knew that if I'd lightly touched her shoulder, or sat opposite and waited she'd look up eventually and reveal dark brown eyes and a mascara streaked face. That she'd have asked what I wanted and that I could have offered to help.

Why didn't I? She'd been a bit of a drama queen, but then who isn't at that age? I'd just walked by. I was just a teenager myself and in no mood for the latest of her daily disasters. Even so... Maybe she'd have said there was nothing wrong, maybe the problem would have been something I couldn't help with. I could have tried though, it might have made a difference.

I never saw my sister again.

Not an hour later she'd stepped off the pavement in front of a speeding car. I didn't see it happen, because I'd walked right by her as she'd sat and cried, left her alone with her misery and carried on with my life. What I did see was a body connected to machines in the hospital. I saw Dad's anger and Mum's worry, but I didn't see my sister. I knew she was already gone from us. We buried her, just after the clocks went back. Nothing else went back to how it should be though. My parents sold the café, moved away, tried to move on.

I started to poke and pry. I wanted, needed, to find a problem I could solve. One which would make it all right. Had I done that with Lucy? Maybe. I had tried at any rate and that made me stronger. Strong enough to take the flowers back past the café where we'd grown up and on to the grave I'd not visited since my sister was lowered into it.

Bright pink lilies were my choice. As vivid a shade as the lipsticks and nail polish she'd worn. As sweetly scented as the lotion she spritzed on her hair before using the tongs. My tongs actually, but I'd never really minded. I sometimes said I did, but she'd known I didn't mean it. She knew I loved her just as I knew…

Then I'm nowhere, I'm floating. I'm nowhere, I'm crushed. Noises. Voices.

"Don't try to move."

I can't anyway.

"I'm a first aider, I'm just going to examine you, OK?"

I don't know if I respond, but I feel hands on my body. Gently I'm moved to what I guess is the recovery position. That's good, I want to recover. Helping Lucy might have allowed me to do that.

"I think you're just winded, but the ambulance is on the way, just to be sure."

He's right. I'd stepped into the road without looking. The driver had swerved but hadn't managed to miss me entirely and I'd been knocked down.

The ambulance comes and the police. I give my name and that of the Prime Minister, and the day of the week. I'm examined and questioned and pronounced to be fine. The car driver too is questioned. She'd stopped. She's sorry. Very, very sorry. She wants to help me, but it isn't me who needs help now, it's her.

"It's OK," I say. "It was just an accident. I had something on my mind and wasn't paying attention, that's all. It wasn't your fault."

"An accident?" I'm not sure if it's the driver's words echoing mine, or my thoughts I hear.

"Yes, just an accident," I say. And it was. I'd not stepped out deliberately, no longer wishing to live. I'd not been blinded by tears or despair. I'd just been thinking about my sister. The sister with whom I'd laughed and joked. Who I'd teased and been tormented by. The sister who'd borrowed my things and lent me hers. Remembering how we'd sometimes helped each other, sometimes been the cause of the problem, how we'd rowed and how we'd loved each other. Thinking that she'd forgive me for the one time I walked by. That it was time to forgive myself.

The driver gives me her name, address and insurance details, just in case. The ambulance staff say I don't need to go to hospital, but everyone seems reluctant to leave me alone.

"Is there someone we can call for you?"

"No. Thank you," I say.

"What about Elizabeth? You were saying her name earlier."

"Elizabeth is my sister. I was on my way... to visit. I bought her some flowers."

The lilies are broken. Quite a mess really, not quite like my tongs had been. I have to sit down. To think, to remember.

My sister sitting at the table, mascara streaked face in her hands, the heated tongs broken apart in front of her. My tongs. One skein of hair still frizzy, the rest perfectly straight.

She'd have had things on her mind as she left the café. Fretting over how she looked. Or maybe she'd sorted it out but made herself late. Or perhaps even guilt that she'd broken something of mine? Whatever it was, it would have distracted her as she stepped out into the road. The car must have been going too fast, everyone had said so. Maybe the driver had more than that to hide as he'd never stopped.

The other driver who, through no fault of hers had hit me, wants to buy more flowers. I say it doesn't matter. I say it through tears, but they aren't the kind I've been hiding away for years, especially around the time the clocks go back. These are the kind of tears which wash away just a little of the pain. The kind I can wipe away before, at last, getting on with my life.

25. Unsweetened Revenge

"Claire dear, you remember we spoke about having our kitchen done?"

Claire did, although it was her mother-in-law who'd done all the talking.

"It will be quite disruptive so we've decided it'll be easier all round if we just come and stay with you for the week."

"Lovely," Claire found the strength to murmur. She was used to her in-laws calling in unannounced or inviting themselves for Sunday lunch even when her husband George was away on duty. Claire didn't mind as she loved to cook and liked that she was treated as family, or at least she wouldn't mind if it weren't for mother-in-law's attitude to the food Claire provided.

Whenever she was offered anything that looked like it might contain more than three calories a pound Mum said something like, "I shouldn't really." She always did grudgingly accept though. After they'd eaten she declared, "We'll all have to do extra exercise after that!"

Dad was different. He happily accepted everything Claire offered, praised her culinary abilities on the rare occasions he had the chance to speak, and looked hopefully at anything still left on the serving plate. George too loved her cooking.

"You're a much better cook than Mum and you allow me to enjoy my food."

"Why on earth wouldn't I?"

George just shrugged leaving Claire sure that his mum's attitude was nothing new. It comforted her a little to know it wasn't personal.

Mum always enquired into the ingredients and made helpful suggestions. Claire was advised she could swap the butter for low fat spread, sugar for sweetener and buy low fat digestives instead of baking chocolate cookies.

Each time Claire nodded thoughtfully and continued to bake using her favourite ingredients. She couldn't see the need for low calorie, low flavour, artificial alternatives. None of them were overweight. OK, Claire could accurately be described as curvy but George liked her that way, her doctor didn't see it as an issue and Claire was happy; except during, and for a while after, Mum's visits.

Claire's mother-in-law claimed she usually avoided dairy products, anything but the leanest meat and all refined carbohydrates. Claire didn't believe her. Her in-laws walked miles, both had jobs where they were on their feet all day and played tennis regularly. That's what kept them slim, not dieting. Besides if she were really so worried about the unhealthy nature of Claire's cooking maybe she should avoid visiting at mealtimes.

A whole week with Mum could be hell, or it could be Claire's chance for revenge.

"It won't work," George warned. "You won't change her. It's the way she was brought up."

When her in-laws arrived Claire greeted them warmly before assuring Mum she needn't worry about putting on weight during the visit.

"Cake and desserts are OK as a treat but not all the time, so I won't be tempting you with anything like that."

Both her in-laws looked disappointed though of course Mum pretended to be pleased.

"Us girls have to be so careful, don't we?" Claire added. "Can't eat like the boys can."

Claire and Mum had unsweetened grapefruit and black coffee for breakfast. Dad and George got eggs and bacon. Claire made and ate some toast in the kitchen as she cooked that.

They all had a Ploughman's salad for lunch. Mum wasn't given any cheese, bread or ham with hers. Claire ate her portions in the kitchen as she prepared the meals then smiled brightly as she placed the super healthy versions in her and Mum's places.

They all had steamed fish and vegetables for dinner. The men also had potatoes and rich buttery sauce and followed that with treacle tart. Mum and Claire had an apple for dessert.

After two days Claire was ravenous despite sneaking extra food in the kitchen. She was grouchy too. If she ate like that all the time she'd make a few mean comments just like Mum. Perhaps it was the woman's obsession with healthy eating that sometimes made her unpleasant?

After four days Mum caught Claire wolfing down a jam sandwich in the kitchen.

"Have you been doing this all week?" she demanded.

Claire admitted it. "I just can't survive on the restrictive diet you want."

"You usually eat what you've been feeding the boys?"

"Slightly smaller portions, but yes the same things."

Mum disappeared into the guest room for an hour, then asked Claire if she could have a word.

"Claire dear, you remember us saying that cakes and things were OK as a treat or for a special occasion?"

Claire did remember saying that.

"I agree with you. I never did before, but I think you're right."

"You do?"

Mum spoke quietly. "Perhaps you could bake one for tea? You're such a wonderful cook and it is a special occasion as we're going home tomorrow. We can celebrate the kitchen being finished and you can celebrate seeing the back of us …"

"Mum, I don't dislike you. I just wish you weren't so critical of my cooking, especially as I know you enjoy eating it."

"I'm sorry. I still feel guilty about enjoying cakes and desserts."

"But why?"

"My mother and sister are both diabetic. They can't eat such things so we never had them at home and I learnt to think of them as dangerous. I never once made George a birthday cake… There's no excuse for taking it out on you, but I'm jealous of how much he likes your cooking."

Claire hugged her mother-in-law.

"Can you forgive me?" Mum asked.

"I can and we will have cake for tea but you're going to bake it. Don't worry, I'll help."

Thank you for reading this book. I hope you enjoyed it. If you did, I'd really appreciate it if you could leave a short review on Amazon and/or Goodreads.

To learn more about my writing life, hear about new releases and get a free short story, sign up to my newsletter – https://mailchi.mp/677f65e1ee8f/sign-up or you can find the link on my website patsycollins.uk

More books by Patsy Collins

Novels –

Firestarter
Escape To The Country
A Year And A Day
Paint Me A Picture
Leave Nothing But Footprints

Non-fiction –

From Story Idea To Reader
(co-written with Rosemary J. Kind)

A Year Of Ideas:
365 sets of writing prompts and exercises

Short story collections –

Over The Garden Fence
Up The Garden Path
Through The Garden Gate
In The Garden Air

No Family Secrets
Can't Choose Your Family
Keep It In The Family
Happy Families

All That Love Stuff
With Love And Kisses
Lots Of Love
Love Is The Answer

Slightly Spooky Stories I
Slightly Spooky Stories II
Slightly Spooky Stories III
Slightly Spooky Stories IV

Just A Job
Perfect Timing
A Way With Words
Dressed To Impress
Coffee & Cake
Not A Drop To Drink

Printed in Great Britain
by Amazon